Without warning, Ethan pulled to him.

He took her mouth as if it was his to do with what he pleased, making it his own in a way that had Jordin's hands rising of their own volition, her fingers curling into his shirt. Her moan slid free of her mouth and into Ethan's.

The kiss was explosive, consuming and intense.

All Jordin could think about was the heat of Ethan's body against her own.

Ethan released her slowly, leaving Jordin breathless, hungry for more of his kisses and drowning in desire.

He drew a slow breath.

She gazed into his chocolate-brown eyes.

"You are irresistible," he murmured, as though having reached some internal understanding with himself. Ethan lowered his head down to hers, and pressed a single kiss on her lips.

Their gazes locked. Jordin and Ethan glimpsed the attraction mirrored in the other's eyes.

Ethan kissed her again, lingering, savoring every moment.

Jord_____er brain,
her_

"I h_____Ethan
wh_____u."

Dear Reader,

Only for You is the second book in the DuGrandpres of Charleston series. Jordin DuGrandpre is thrilled that Ethan Holbrooke is back in Charleston. She intends to seize this opportunity for the two of them to reconnect. However, Jordin finds that she has to knock down the wall around Ethan's heart.

I was inspired to write this story during a visit to Charleston, South Carolina. While there, I overheard a snippet of a conversation about a young woman who was perplexed by the actions of a friend who recently returned home. There is a saying that "home is where the heart is," and for Ethan, this is true.

Best,

Jacquelin

ONLY
FOR YOU

JACQUELIN
THOMAS

HHARLEQUIN®KIMANI™ROMANCE

Recycling programs
for this product may
not exist in your area.

ISBN-13: 978-0-373-86482-9

Only for You

Copyright © 2016 by Jacquelin Thomas

HHARLEQUIN®
™ www.Harlequin.com

Printed in U.S.A.

Jacquelin Thomas is an award-winning, bestselling author with more than fifty-five books in print. When not writing, she is busy catching up on her reading, attending sporting events and spoiling her grandchildren. Jacquelin and her family live in North Carolina.

Books by Jacquelin Thomas

Harlequin Kimani Romance

Visit the Author Profile page
at Harlequin.com for more titles.

Bernard, you are my best friend and the love of my life.
My heart is always with you.

Chapter 1

Jordin DuGrandpre stared out her office window, immersed in sights and sounds of the downtown business district. In 1960, her grandfather Marcelle founded the first African American–owned law firm in Charleston, South Carolina. DuGrandpre Law Offices was in its new location, four floors above bustling Broad Street. Marcelle's esteemed legacy had continued with twin sons Etienne and Jacques DuGrandpre and their children.

Etienne's daughter Jordin loved this city of her birth and could never imagine living anywhere else. She adored everything about Charleston—the waterfront park, the food…everything.

"I guess you heard the news about Boot Camp Gym."

Turning away from her office view of downtown, Jordin faced her twin sister. "Jadin, I didn't hear you come in," she stated.

"I noticed." She gestured toward the window. "This view is absolutely stunning."

Jordin gave a slight nod of agreement. "I did hear about the new gym. I actually went by there a few days ago. I'm really happy for Ethan." She felt a warm glow flow through her.

Jadin sat down in one of the visitor chairs. "I am too," she murmured. "It's good to see how things worked out for him."

"Ethan had a lot going on back then—more than any of us knew." Jordin and Ethan Holbrooke had been friends since they were in middle school. She still remembered the day he left as if it had been yesterday, although eleven years had passed. She had been sixteen at the time and heartbroken over losing her best friend.

"Are you still infatuated with him?" Jadin inquired, leaning forward in her seat, looking at Jordin as if she were trying to figure out what she was thinking. "You don't have to say anything because I'm sure I already know the answer to that question."

"I will always care about Ethan."

A grin spread across her sister's face. "*I knew it*. You still have feelings for him."

Jordin stared into golden-brown eyes that mirrored her own. "Drop it, Jadin. I haven't seen Ethan in a long time. Besides, I'm sure he's forgotten all about me. Especially since he never once tried to contact me after he left." She swallowed the hurt she felt behind Ethan's actions. He had promised to keep in touch no matter what.

"But you haven't forgotten about him though." Jadin's voice pulled Jordin away from her thoughts.

She did not confirm or deny her sister's statement.

"Have you heard if he's moving back here or just opening the gym?" Jadin inquired.

"I haven't," she responded, "but I'm hoping that he will come back to Charleston to stay. I've missed him."

"This man is not the same boy and teenager you remember, Jordin. Besides, he may be married with a family. I don't want you getting hurt."

She detected a hint of censure in her sister's tone. "He's not married," Jordin announced. "It was mentioned in another article I came across."

"But it doesn't mean that he's exactly free and single either," Jadin countered.

"I know…" she responded with a soft sigh. "It's not like I'm planning a wedding or setting my hopes and dreams on Ethan. I just want to reconnect with him. There's nothing wrong with that."

"Not as long as your expectations are realistic."

A tall, slender woman dressed in a pair of navy blue pants and a crisp powder-blue blouse appeared in the doorway.

"Mom, what are you doing here on a Monday?" Jordin asked. The only time Eleanor usually came by the office was for a weekly lunch date with her husband on Wednesdays.

"Your father wanted to see me," she responded. "He just informed me that another DuGrandpre is joining the firm."

Jordin noted her mother did not seem thrilled by the news. "Is it Andre? He's been talking about leaving New Orleans for a while now." Eleanor did not care much for her nephew's choice in the criminals he often represented. In truth, Jordin felt the same way about her cousin.

Eleanor shook her head no. "It's not Andre."

"Then who is it?" Jadin inquired.

"Your brother." Eleanor's tone was coolly disapproving.

"Austin is coming to Charleston," Jordin uttered in

surprise. "I wonder how his mother feels about his decision to work with Dad." Her father was married briefly to a woman named Irene and Austin was born out of that union.

When Etienne DuGrandpre married Jordin's mother, Irene left Charleston vowing that Etienne would never see his son again. Although she could not manipulate the court system in her favor, Irene was successful in alienating her son from his father by making him believe that Etienne loved his twin daughters more. By the time he was sixteen, Austin wanted little to do with his father.

"How does Dad feel about this?" Jordin questioned.

"He's ecstatic, of course. This is something he's always wanted."

"Mom, how do you feel about this?" Jadin wanted to know.

"I'm not sure," Eleanor responded candidly. "I just find it interesting that a man who has had nothing to do with his father for years suddenly wants to work in the family law firm. I'm suspicious of his motives."

"I have to admit I'm feeling the same way," Jordin confessed. "I was surprised when I heard that Austin decided to study law and now this…" She gave a slight shrug. "I don't know. Maybe he really wants to connect with the father he barely knew."

Eleanor sat down in the empty chair next to Jadin. "Your father tried to be there for Austin but was rejected at every turn. His mother turned him against his own father. It still angers me to think of it." She retained her affability, but there was a distinct hardening of her eyes.

"Austin's a grown man," Jadin stated. "Maybe he's ready to repair his relationship with Dad. He may not have any ulterior motives."

"All we can do is wait and see how this goes," Eleanor stated. "I just don't want your father to be disappointed."

Jordin nodded in agreement as she checked her watch. "I have to go. I need to head over to the courthouse to meet with my client. I'll give you a call later, Mom." She began placing documents into her tote.

"I think I'll go with you," Jadin said. "I haven't seen you in action in a while. Besides, I want to see how this case goes."

"I believe in our justice system, so I'm sure my client will win. We have a lot of strong evidence to support his claims."

"I'll go get my purse."

Jordin grabbed her tote, and then said, "Meet me at the car. I am going to walk down with Mom."

Jadin rose to her feet. "I'll be right behind you."

Eleanor looped her arm through Jordin's. "I hope you are not spending all of your free time alone."

"I'm not, Mom. I'm not dating anyone, but I still manage to get out with friends and have a good time."

"I know that you want to have a husband and family at some point—it won't happen unless you meet someone."

Jordin smiled. "I don't just want to meet any man, Mom. I want the right one." As far as she was concerned, there was only one man perfect for her. The problem was that she hadn't heard from him in years.

Ethan Holbrooke's head was throbbing when he woke, and he felt nauseated. After the feeling passed, he shook the foggy feeling in his head and swallowed to rid the cottony taste from his mouth as he sat up in bed.

Charleston. The very place he'd vowed never to return to eleven years ago. So what had prompted him to open his newest gym in a city that evoked bad memories?

Jordin DuGrandpre.

Eleven years away from her and Jordin was as fresh in his mind as she had been when he was taken away from Charleston. They had been sixteen years old at the time. He recalled that she had tears in her eyes as they said their goodbyes. Ethan promised to keep in touch, but did not keep his word. It was too painful, and at the time, he doubted he would ever see Jordin again.

Ethan had intentionally avoided all contact with her because he did not relish seeing the pity in her eyes, or hearing it in her voice. After all, he was not a victim. He survived his mother's abandonment, his father's rejection and the rigorous training at the military academy. When he graduated college, Ethan sold weight loss products from the trunk of his car by posting handmade flyers all over Richmond, Virginia. In the first month, he made five thousand dollars and three years later, he was a millionaire. Now, Ethan owned a chain of fifteen gyms around the country.

He shook away his thoughts and hustled to take a shower. He had an appointment to meet with a news reporter to discuss his latest gym and its programs.

An hour later, Ethan stalked through the entrance with his jaw clenched. His scowl wasn't aimed at anyone or anything particular. Ethan hated giving interviews, but considered it crucial to his business.

The woman was already there when he arrived.

Running her fingers through her blond curls, she awarded him a huge smile as he approached her. "Thank you for meeting me, Mr. Holbrooke. I'm Helen Jovanovich."

"Just call me Ethan."

"Okay, Ethan. I really appreciate you taking time out of your busy schedule to talk to me."

He unlocked the double doors and escorted her inside.

"Wow," she murmured. "This is unlike any other gym I've seen before."

"This is something I hear all of the time," Ethan responded. "This is what makes Holbrooke Boot Camp Gyms different from any other. Our programs are designed for people who are really serious about exercise. The training is rigorous."

"In what way?" Helen asked as she scribbled words in a notebook.

"We have a total body circuit training that can burn eight hundred to twelve hundred calories a session using various pieces of equipment. This program is never the same routine." Ethan paused a moment before continuing. "This is our Suspension Trainer. It's a highly versatile piece of equipment that uses a person's own body weight to build functional strength and improve flexibility, balance and core stability all at once."

"So the programs here are definitely not for those who dabble in exercise."

"They are for people who are serious about fitness," Ethan emphasized. "Our martial arts and circuit training class is designed to train a person like a fighter. We have several professional athletes who train regularly with us in the off-season."

Helen touched one of the one-hundred-pound heavy bags. "I can certainly see why. What do you call this?"

"These are our ground and pound bags. They are six feet tall and weigh a hundred pounds or more."

"So all of your programs are designed to push you to your limits?"

"Yes," Ethan stated. "Customers come to Boot Camp Gym because they want to learn advanced weight training techniques."

"I see that you offer a kickboxing class."

He nodded. "My kickboxing program is a high-intensity training technique using multiple tools on the heavy bag."

Ethan released a sigh of relief when the interview came to an end. He left the reporter in the care of his new gym manager, but he wasn't ready to return to his hotel suite. He had been away from Charleston for a long time. It was time to get reacquainted with the city.

An hour later, Ethan lost himself in the rhythmic sounds of the churning wheels of his bike as he rounded the first bend of a ten-mile ride. He enjoyed the feel of the cool air on his face as he rode, pushing himself hard to help take the edge off his mood, but so far it hadn't helped.

Jordin hummed softly as she strolled into the lobby of the building where she worked. She was joined a few minutes later by an associate. "Good morning, Keith."

"Morning," the man uttered in response with his jaw clenched.

She knew that his scowl wasn't aimed at anyone or anything in particular, but she did not try to initiate him in conversation. Jordin moved out of his way as he stabbed the elevator control panel. Keith was a brilliant lawyer and charismatic in the courtroom. Outside of this, he was not necessarily a people person.

The elevator doors slid open minutes later to reveal the reception desk and waiting area of the DuGrandpre Law Offices. Keith's nod to the receptionist was curt but polite as he moved past her toward his office.

Jordin smiled. "Good morning, Charlotte."

The woman smiled in return. "It's always nice to see your sunny smile, especially after a cloud blows through."

She knew Charlotte was referring to Keith and chuckled softly. "Be nice…"

Jordin stopped in front of her father's secretary. "Is my dad in yet?" She asked as her fingers drummed distractedly on the desk.

"He should be here within the hour."

"Okay, thanks."

Humming softly, Jordin made her way to her office, shutting the door behind her.

Ethan was opening a gym in Charleston. It was a great opportunity to try to reconnect with him, she considered. Then she could find out why he hadn't kept his promise to stay in contact.

She sighed softly.

Jordin missed her best friend and longed to see him again, but it was best not to get her hopes up. The pain in her heart was like an old wound that ached on a rainy day.

Her thoughts were interrupted by the ringing of her telephone.

It was her father's secretary.

"Your father has arrived and he would like to see you."

"I'll be right there, Charlotte."

Jordin left her office and walked the short distance to the large corner suite. "Good morning, Dad."

Etienne smiled warmly. "I heard you were fantastic in court yesterday."

She sat down in one of the visitor chairs. "I believed that my client was the best choice to raise his son and the judge agreed in light of the evidence." Jordin paused a moment before adding, "I felt bad for the mother though, but she still has a lot to do before she can handle parenting."

"How is the boy?"

Jordin smiled. "He's happy. His mother will have supervised visitation every other weekend once she completes rehab."

Her father nodded in approval. "That child's happiness and safety is what is most important."

She agreed.

A slender woman strolled into Etienne's office without knocking.

"Good morning, Aunt Rochelle," Jordin greeted.

A flash of annoyance crossed her father's face. She knew that he only tolerated Rochelle out of respect for his brother. His sister-in-law was a great attorney, but otherwise a selfish and inconsiderate person.

"Hello, dear," Rochelle responded. "You were on my mind last night, Jordin. I'm really surprised that you haven't gotten married already. You're pretty enough and I know how much you love children—"

Jordin quickly rose to her feet, and cut her off by saying, "I don't want to hold you up so I'll leave so you can talk with Dad."

"Hon, can you drop these off with Ryker?" Rochelle asked, holding a thick folder.

"Sure." Jordin cast a look of sympathy at her father before exiting his office. Her aunt had a good heart but she was snobbish, opinionated and very protective of her children. When Ryker and Garland first got married, her interference almost ruined their relationship.

Jordin walked briskly down the hall to where Ryker's office was located. "These are from your mother."

"Hey, did you know that Ethan is back in town, cousin?" he inquired when Jordin set the folder containing legal documents on his desk.

She felt a warm glow flow through her body and responded, "No, I didn't know he was here. Have you see him?"

He shook his head no. "Garland and I ran into Chandler Morris last night while having dinner. He told us that Ethan was moving back permanently."

"That's great news about Ethan," she murmured. "I'd really like to see him."

Ryker didn't blink when he looked at Jordin and broke the news. "Then you'll be thrilled to know that he's moving his corporate offices here, as well. His office is in the building on the corner."

Jordin's heart sang with delight. "Now that I know where his office is located, maybe I'll drop by with a gift to welcome him back to Charleston, and then I'll fuss him out for not keeping his promise to me."

Ryker gave her a knowing smile. "Why am I not surprised?"

She folded her arms across her chest. "I'm going to forgive him because he has always been my best friend. I can't wait to see Ethan again."

"I understand. I'd like to see him as well."

"We can go there together," Jordin suggested.

Ryker shook his head no. "I'm sure you'd like to have some time alone to get reacquainted with Ethan."

Her smile broadened in approval.

"Oh, before I forget, the girls want to spend some time with you this weekend," he announced. "What's your schedule like?"

"I don't have anything special planned. Why don't I come get them Friday after work and keep them until Sunday? You and Garland can have some couple time."

"You don't have to do that."

Jordin met her cousin's gaze. "I *want* to do this. I love spending time with Kai and Amya."

"Maybe you can explain to them that while they have

the same birthday, they are not twins. They know that you and Jadin are twins as well as my dad and your dad."

She laughed. "They are just trying to figure all this out."

"Garland and I tried to explain that they are not twins because they have different mothers."

"Ryker, they are only four years old. Amya never knew her biological mother—all she knows is that Garland is her mom. She is also the only mother Kai has known. When they are older, they will understand that they were switched at birth and how it worked out in the end."

"Happily-ever-after," Ryker murmured.

Jordin broke into a smile. "I love seeing you so happy."

"I love Garland more and more each day. She is a wonderful wife and mother."

"You complement each other."

"I've always felt that way about you and Ethan," Ryker told her. "Remember how you two used to finish each other's sentences?"

Jordin chuckled. "Yeah, we did do that."

"When you see him, don't forget to give him my regards."

"I won't. Thanks for the heads-up on Ethan," Jordin said as she headed toward the door.

Although she was happy to hear that her best friend had returned, troubling thoughts assailed her. *Ethan's back and he didn't even try to contact me. Eleven years have gone by and no word from him. Why didn't he keep his promise?*

Jordin had such a warm, loving spirit and she was always smiling. Ethan loved her sense of humor and the sense of freedom she seemed to have in her life. Not only was she beautiful but she was intelligent as well. There had always been an undeniable magnetism between them, which probably explained why he was sitting in a parked vehicle across the street from the law firm, watching as she and Jadin walked to the bistro located on the corner.

Coward.

Ethan had missed her greatly but was unsure of the best way to approach her, especially after he hadn't bothered to stay in contact with her over the years. He knew that in deciding to move back to Charleston, they would run into each other eventually.

But as strong as his attraction was to Jordin, Ethan knew that he could never act on those feelings. A relationship other than friendship between them could never work because they were from two very different worlds. But also because love was not a part of his plans for the future. He was focused on his company and didn't have the time or the inclination to deviate from the driving force that had been guiding him since college.

Ethan pulled up the collar of his jacket and turned the key in the ignition. He drove to his hotel. The home he purchased would not be ready for another two weeks.

He sat down in the living area of his suite and picked up the television remote. Jordin was still at the forefront of his mind. He considered calling her at the office, but decided to wait until he found the right words to say to her.

Ethan tried watching TV, but when he couldn't find anything to his liking; he gave up and reached for a magazine on health and exercise trends.

He was interrupted an hour later when his friend Chandler called.

"How did your interview go?"

"Okay," Ethan responded. "It's just not something I

enjoy doing. I'm thinking of hiring someone to handle publicity."

"Have you talked to Ryker or Jordin?"

"Not yet," he answered. "I've been so busy with the gym…"

"You might as well know that I told Ryker you were in town."

"That means that Jordin knows as well," Ethan uttered. "She was going to find out eventually, I guess."

"Her knowing is not such a bad thing, is it?"

"No."

"Have you visited any of the old haunts?"

"I did a ride-by on my bike a couple of times," Ethan confessed, "but that's about it. I didn't go by my old neighborhood though."

"Are you worried that you'll run into your mom? My aunt said that she saw her at the market last Saturday."

Ethan swallowed his surprise. He'd had no idea that Lydia was back in Charleston. "She's the least of my worries."

"I'm sure she's heard by now that you were moving back."

He chose his words carefully. "It doesn't matter to me. She's not a part of my life anymore." Ethan changed the subject by asking, "What time are we meeting for dinner tomorrow night?"

Their conversation ended ten minutes later after setting a time to meet.

He got up and made his way to the master bathroom where he showered and put on a pair of sweats.

Jordin.

He found himself wanting to open up to her about everything, but to feel her pity was much more than Ethan could bear. He had no idea how much she'd heard about that awful period of his life, but staying away from Jordin would not be easy, especially when his new office was a block away from the DuGrandpre firm.

Chapter 2

I have no business being here, Jordin thought as she strolled through the doors of the 4200 Broad Street building where Ethan's new offices were located. She'd debated most of the morning whether to show up at his place of business. Although Jordin had not heard from him, she decided to take the initiative.

She'd chosen a black-and-white color-blocked dress with a pair of red shoes and red accessories for work today. *I always get compliments whenever I wear this outfit.* Jordin imagined her look would also garner Ethan's attention.

A sense of pride flowed through her as her eyes traveled around the lobby area with a two-story atrium filled with large vases of flowers and a stunning collection of abstract artwork. Ethan had chosen a great location for his home office.

She followed the sign to the elevators and took one to the top floor.

The elevator doors slid open.

She walked down the short hallway to the penthouse suite.

Jordin entered with determination through the double doors that led to the reception desk and waiting area of Ethan's company.

She smiled at the receptionist, but caught sight of the man she longed to see. "Ethan?"

Their gazes locked across the room. Jordin noted the brief reaction of shock and pleasure in his chocolate-brown eyes before it faded into a businesslike stare.

Ethan excused himself from the person he was talking to and quickly walked toward her.

Smiling, Jordin met him halfway.

He looked so good. She gave him a quick and not-so-subtle once-over. Ethan was no longer the scrawny boy she remembered. He had grown taller and was built solid like a military tank. She doubted there was an ounce of fat anywhere on his body. He was all muscle. However, his movements were fluid and agile.

The words, "Hey, stranger, what are you doing here?" popped out of his mouth almost immediately.

"I've been here all along," she replied smoothly. "It's you who disappeared without a word. Then you come back into town and I don't even get a phone call." Jordin tried to maintain her cordial tone.

She heard his sharp intake of breath.

"You're right," Ethan said after a moment. "Things were crazy for me back then and I didn't want to involve you in that madness. As for now, I had every intention of reconnecting with you, but as you can probably understand, it's been a busy time for me."

Jordin broke into a smile. "I'm glad you decided to come home. I have missed you so much."

The tenderness in Ethan's expression amazed her. "I missed you too."

Her only emotion was relief.

Jordin glanced around. She could feel the heat of the receptionist's gaze on them.

"How about a tour of your new office?" she suggested in a low voice.

"I have to warn you that there's still a lot of work left to be done," Ethan told her as he escorted her down the hall. "I guess we'll start with my office."

"Did your employees relocate here with you?"

"Most of them did," he responded. "I was quite surprised because I hadn't expected so many to want to leave Virginia."

As soon as Jordin walked into his office, she said, "I don't know what you were talking about, Ethan. This place is amazing."

She loved the contemporary look. Ethan had combined leather and fabric furnishings for a unique, yet professional representation of his company. The camouflage chairs looked to be custom designed.

"The furnishings are from my old office," Ethan explained. "I think it's time for something new."

"I think it fits your Boot Camp Gym branding."

Jordin swallowed past the dryness in her throat, her hungry gaze taking him in. He wore a suit, black with faint pinstripes running through the expensive fabric; a crisp, pale gray shirt and a perfectly knotted burgundy tie. Ethan's eyes were a rich, dark brown and his caramel-tinted face had chiseled features with a strong jaw. Everything about the man sizzled with sensuality.

Once inside with the doors closed, he said, "I'm sorry

about that, Jordin. I want you to know that I regret not staying in contact with you."

His intense gaze made her breath go ragged. "So why didn't you call or write me?"

"At the time, I thought it was best."

She embraced him, surprising them both. "It was a long time ago."

"A lifetime ago," Ethan responded as he held her close. "From the looks of it, you were too busy to miss me. I hear you're a force to be reckoned with in the courtroom."

Stepping away from him, Jordin broke into a smile. "I don't know about that, but I do fight tooth and nail for my clients."

He gestured for her to sit down in the green leather chair near the window. "It's what you always wanted."

Ethan sat down in the other one.

"It's in my blood," Jordin responded as she settled against the chair cushion. "You're the one who's doing big things around here. I've read all about your success. Ethan, I'm so proud of you."

"I found something I was passionate about and things just kind of took off from there."

"I'm going to have to check out your gym."

His eyes slid casually over her body. "The programs are rigorous."

"What are you trying to say, Ethan?" Jordin asked with a grin. "You don't think I can handle your boot camp program?"

"It's intense. Do you believe you're up to the challenge?" he questioned.

Jordin met his gaze. "Definitely."

"The gym will be open in a couple of weeks," Ethan announced. "I guess we'll find out what you're made of then."

She laughed.

"How is your family?" he inquired.

"They're great," Jordin responded. "How about your mother? Have you two been in contact since you've been back?"

Ethan's smile disappeared as he walked over to his mahogany desk and stared down at his reflection in the uncluttered surface. "She's the last person I expect or want to hear from," he stated in a curt tone.

Jordin was stunned by the look of loathing on his face. It was clear that he held a lot of resentment against the woman who had abandoned him. She swallowed hard before saying, "I'm sorry to hear that."

"Don't be," he uttered. "I'm not."

She stared, wordlessly. Jordin could not believe he was talking about his mother like that. At one time, the two shared a very close relationship.

"I know it sounds harsh, but I see no point in pretending."

Jordin wanted to ask what happened after he left Charleston, but had a feeling this was not the right time. They would have the chance to have that conversation in time.

Finally, she said, "I'm just happy you decided to come back home, Ethan."

"It was not my original intent," he confessed. "But now that I'm here…seeing you again…it's all good."

"Deep down, I always believed that you would return," Jordin stated.

As their eyes met, she felt a cold shock run through her.

"To be honest, I vowed never to return to this place."

"This is just more evidence that I'm always right," she responded, wanting to lighten the mood.

Ethan chuckled. "That statement proves just how wrong you are."

"You have always been a sore loser."

They both laughed.

Jordin glanced down at her watch. "Ethan, I need to get to court, but I wanted to come by and see you."

"I'm glad that you did. It's good to see you."

Ethan walked her out of the building and to her car. He handed her a business card. "Text me your phone number."

"Definitely," she responded with a smile. "I'm thrilled you're back."

Jordin stared with longing at him before getting in and turning the key in the ignition.

Ethan's really back. Jordin had to see him for herself before she actually believed it. His return was an answer to her prayers.

Upon her arrival at the courthouse minutes later, Jordin parked her car, and then texted her cell and home numbers to Ethan. She anticipated hearing from him within a few days. The prolonged anticipation was almost unbearable.

Ethan's obvious resentment of his mother was still at the forefront of Jordin's mind. She shared a close relationship with her family, although she understood that his situation, like many others was a different experience. It was one of the reasons she chose to specialize in family law. She also volunteered at a women's shelter twice a week and offered pro bono services to families who could not afford legal fees. She worked to keep as many families together as possible.

Her heart ached over Ethan's pain. Jordin could not fully comprehend how a mother could just abandon her child like that. When they were younger, Ethan once told her that he suspected his mother's boyfriend, Rob, was a drug dealer. Like Ethan, Jordin did not care for him and had no idea why Lydia was so in love with someone like Rob. He was controlling, possessive and verbally abusive to both Lydia and Ethan.

Jordin often wondered if Lydia was still with Rob, and if their life together was worth the price of abandoning her own child. It was obvious that Ethan was still angry with her for leaving him.

I would probably be just as angry if I were in his shoes, she thought. Despite his feelings, Ethan had decided to return home, and for that, Jordin was ecstatic.

The scent of Jordin was beyond description. The connection was still alive and sizzling between them. It had not been shattered by time apart.

He needed to get a grip, Ethan scolded silently, but it was hard to do because the floral perfume Jordin wore still lingered in the air, although she had already left his office.

She was no longer the gangly teenage girl he remembered; she had grown into a beautiful woman. Her walk still had a sunny cheerfulness. Ethan had always loved how Jordin's features became animated whenever she discussed a subject she was passionate about. She had become more stylish and glamorous in her choice of clothing—a huge difference from the teenage girl with an obsession for Bedazzled denim jeans and T-shirts.

"You just missed your mother's call," the receptionist announced when he returned to his office.

"If she calls me back, just take a message," he stated without emotion.

Lydia Holbrooke was the main reason Ethan briefly considered not relocating to Charleston, but he put aside

his personal feelings in favor of a smart business decision. Besides, at the time, Ethan had no idea where she
was. Resentment over her abandonment still filled his
heart.

Ethan leaned back in his chair and let out a frustrated
growl. Lydia being back in Charleston was indifferent to
him. One thing for sure, he was not about to let her sabo-
tage everything he had worked for in his life.

He was the result of his mother's affair with a man
who was engaged to another woman.

Despite Lydia's pregnancy, his father's fiancée decided
to go through with the wedding, although she made it
clear that she wanted nothing to do with Ethan. He and
his mother were close until she met Rob Calloway. Rob
was possessive and jealous. He didn't want Lydia to spend
time with her own child.

His mother always warned him of the dangers of drugs
and alcohol, which Ethan considered hypocritical on her
part because the man she was so in love with sold drugs
for a living. In the end, she and Rob were arrested in
Maryland for transporting drugs across state lines. His
mother went to prison while he had to move to North
Carolina to live with the father he barely knew.

His stepmother made it obvious that she was not happy
with him being in her home. She did not want him around
his siblings. His father apologized before sending him
away to attend a military academy in Virginia.

He spent most of his holidays with the families of
school friends, vowing never to return where he was
clearly not welcomed. Ethan swallowed hard, forcing
down the bitterness that threatened to spill out.

He leaned back in his chair to think. Ethan remained
that way for a few moments, and then sat up. Instead of

thinking of the past, his time would be better spent focusing on the future of his company.

Jordin hummed as she prepared a simple dinner of meat loaf and mashed potatoes. She checked her phone several times, hoping that Ethan had tried to contact her.

After she finished eating, Jordin cleaned up the kitchen before settling down for the evening. She felt a wave of disappointment that she had not heard from Ethan. It was clear that he wasn't as eager to talk to her as she had imagined he would be. Jordin sighed, clasped her hands together and stared at them.

He had seemed happy enough to see her, however.

Jordin considered calling Ethan, but she had already made the initial contact—the ball was now in Ethan's court.

She had always believed that Ethan had feelings toward her, although those emotions never bloomed into anything more than friendship. He hadn't changed all that much outside of the huge chip on his shoulder. Jordin had done her best to put Ethan out of her mind over the years, but he held a permanent spot in her heart.

Her sister's suggestion that he was possibly involved with someone came back to haunt her. Jordin could not imagine their friendship coming to an end because of his relationship with another woman. The idea of Ethan in love with anyone but her filled her with jealousy. Jordin had always believed he would come back to Charleston— back to her.

Chapter 3

Jordin glanced over at the desk calendar in her office, sighing in frustration. Five days had passed and still not a word from Ethan. She continued to put off calling him. Despite her frustration, Jordin was determined to wait for him to make contact. In the meantime, she kept herself busy.

She and Jadin had made plans to spend the day shopping. Her sister was expected to arrive at any moment.

The doorbell sounded, putting an end to her musings.

Jordin opened her door fully expecting to see her sister. She gasped in surprise. "Austin..." She had no idea that her brother was already in Charleston, but seeing him at her door thrilled Jordin beyond words.

"Hey, little sister."

"When did you get into town?"

"Thursday night," he responded. "Can you pretend to be a little happy to see me?"

"Oh, I'm glad that you're here," Jordin replied. "I was just surprised to find you at the door. I was expecting Jadin and I thought you were her. C'mon inside." She stepped aside to allow her brother entrance into her home.

"Good, I want to talk to you both."

She studied his expression for a moment before asking, "Is everything okay, Austin?"

He nodded. "Yeah."

The room enveloped in uneasy silence.

"I heard Ryker got married again," Austin stated, breaking the quiet.

"He did," Jordin confirmed, "and they have two beautiful daughters and another baby on the way. They recently found out that this one is a boy."

"I'm happy for him."

Another pregnant pause.

"Austin, I'm ecstatic to hear that you are joining us at the firm." Jordin broke into a smile. "You have to know that it's a dream come true for Dad."

He did not respond.

"How is your mother?" she asked.

"She's great."

"How does she feel about your coming here and working with Dad?"

"She's not thrilled about it," Austin admitted candidly, "but it was my decision to make."

"It's really going to be nice having you around," Jordin stated.

The doorbell sounded.

"This has to be Jadin," she announced. She walked briskly across the hardwood floor and opened the door.

Her sister entered the house. "Are you ready to go?"

Jadin's eyes strayed over to where her brother was

sitting. "Austin, I had no idea you were here. When did you arrive in town?"

"I've been here since Thursday evening."

"You've been in town for a day and a half and we are just now hearing from you. Why is that?" Jadin questioned.

"I spent yesterday looking for a place to live. I'd like to get settled as soon as I can before I start work."

"Austin, what's the real reason you came to Charleston?" Jadin wanted to know. "I know that it wasn't just because you wanted to be close to Dad."

"Actually, it has everything to do with him," he responded. "I want to get to know Etienne DuGrandpre for myself. I need to see if he's anything like my mother said."

Jadin smiled at him. "I think that's a smart decision."

Jordin wasn't so sure that she believed Austin. She clung to the idea that there was another reason for his coming to Charleston. One that he obviously wasn't willing to share with his sisters.

"Well, I'll head out since you two already have plans."

"You're welcome to join us," Jordin stated, "but I have to warn you—we love to shop."

He smiled. "Maybe next time."

Jordin and Jadin each gave him a hug before walking out with him.

"Well, big brother is in town," Jadin murmured as she settled into her sister's car.

Jordin nodded. "Yeah, but I don't think this is just about Dad."

"So what do you think the real reason could be?"

"I have no idea," Jordin responded. "My instincts are telling me that he also came to Charleston for another purpose."

"Well, we will find out what his motives are in time."
Changing the subject, Jadin said, "Ryker told me that you
went to see Ethan. How did that go?"

"Fine," she answered. "I was so happy to see him. Sis,
he is so handsome."

"He's always been nice looking."
Jordin agreed.

Fifteen minutes later, they strolled through the doors
of a downtown fashion boutique.

"I know that you really care about Ethan, but maybe
you should keep some distance between the two of you,"
Jadin suggested as she switched her purse from one
shoulder to the other.

"It's not like he came looking for you when he returned to Charleston."

Her words stung, but Jordin kept her expression blank.
"No, he did not contact me, but Ethan's still my friend and
I'm not going to abandon him. He's been through a lot."

"You can't save him."

She turned and met her sister's gaze straight on. "I'm
just trying to reconnect with my friend. That's all."

"I don't think even you believe that," her sister responded.

"Seriously," Jordin uttered. "This is about friendship."

Changing the subject, she asked, "What do you think
of this dress?"

Jadin smiled and nodded in approval. "I love it."

"So do I," Jordin responded. She was glad to put an
end to discussing Ethan. She and Jadin would never agree
when it came to him.

After forty minutes in the store, they were finally
satisfied with their selections. Jordin led the way to the
cash register.

"I spent more than I'd planned, but I found some great buys," she said, pulling out her credit card.

"There were some great items on sale," Jadin agreed.

Purchases in hand, they headed to the exit door a few minutes later.

Jordin heard a familiar voice shortly after they stepped outside. She looked over her shoulder, then stopped in her tracks.

"Hello, ladies…"

"Hello, Ethan," she and Jadin replied in unison.

He chuckled at their response. "Still doing the twin thing, I see."

Jordin laughed. "Since we're identical, I don't think that's ever going to change."

Ethan's smile warmed her.

"I didn't expect to run into you," Jordin stated.

"It's Saturday and the day is beautiful," he responded. "I thought I'd enjoy some of it."

Jadin gave a slight nod. "It's a really nice day."

Ethan met Jordin's gaze and said, "I'd planned to call you, but this was a really hectic week for me. I had to fly out to Arizona for business, and then Memphis for a conference."

"I understand," she murmured. Deep down, Jordin felt a measure of relief upon hearing the reasons why Ethan had not called. She was beginning to wonder if he was avoiding her.

"Do you have any plans for this evening?" he inquired.

"I'm having a girls' night at my place."

He laughed. "I definitely don't want to interfere with that."

Jordin chuckled. "No, you don't."

"How about I give you a call tomorrow night?"

She broke into a smile. "I look forward to talking to

you then." Ethan glanced over at Jadin and added, "It's good seeing you again."

"Same here," she responded.

Ethan gave Jordin a quick hug, and then hugged her sister before leaving them to enjoy their shopping.

"You were right," Jadin stated. "Ethan is very handsome and so muscular."

"I told you…"

"He seems a little distant though."

"Really?" Jordin asked. "I don't think so."

"Be careful, sis."

"I don't know why you and Dad dislike Ethan so much. He's never done anything to anyone in our family."

"I can't speak for our father, but I personally have nothing against the man," Jadin stated. "I just know that your feelings run pretty deep where he is concerned and I don't want to see you get hurt."

"That's just it, Jadin. I don't have anything to worry about where Ethan is concerned. He is a good person."

"I don't doubt that. I'm just not sure he cares for you as much as you care for him."

Jordin eyed her sister. "I know what I'm doing."

"I hope so," Jadin replied. "I really hope so."

Her sister never took the time to really get to know him when they were younger. She decided to change the subject by saying, "I'm picking up Amya and Kai this evening."

"Oooh. I haven't seen them in a couple of weeks."

"Why don't you come by tonight?" Jordin suggested. "We can make it a real girls' night."

"Michael will be back today. We're going to have dinner together. If it's not too late afterward, I'll try to swing by to see them."

Jadin and Michael had dated in law school. While she

did not care for the man personally, Jordin was careful not to interfere in her sister's relationship. She only wished her sister would give her the same respect.

Ethan pulled up to a stoplight and waited patiently for the light to change. He felt guilty. He should've called Jordin by now, but he kept putting it off. He hated avoiding her, but for now, Ethan felt it was for the best.

He felt the tiny hairs on the back of his neck stand up.

Ethan glanced out the window, his eyes landing on a pretty woman sitting in the car next to him. She smiled at him and gave a little wave.

He returned her smile out of politeness.

The light changed and Ethan was on his way. He harbored no regret at not getting her name and number. He had no time for romantic relationships.

Ethan pulled into a parking space fifteen minutes later. He got out of the car, grabbed a stack of documents and headed to the entrance of his new gym.

The manager was in his office when Ethan walked inside.

"Hey, Walter," he greeted. "I wanted to touch base with you about the grand opening. Here are copies of the new ads coming out this week."

Walter scanned through the pages. "Nice…"

"Are the showers fully installed?" Ethan questioned.

"All of the bathrooms and showers are all ready to go. The childcare center is almost complete. The painters should be here later today."

"Looks like everything is right on schedule."

Walter nodded. "The uniforms are due to arrive tomorrow."

"What about the member T-shirts? When are they supposed to come in?"

"By the end of the week. I spoke to Allen and he can send us some if we need them sooner."

Allen was the gym manager in Virginia. Ethan met him when he was a trainer at another company. Allen was the first employee Ethan hired to work at his first gym. He became a manager three years later.

Ethan left the gym two hours later to meet Chandler at a restaurant for dinner.

"I can't believe I let you talk me into moving back to Charleston," he stated after they were seated in a booth with a view of the waterfront. "You know when I left this town—I vowed never to return."

He and Chandler had been best friends since kindergarten. Ethan had corresponded with him a few times over the years, but they had talked more frequently in the past six months.

"This is about business," Chandler responded. "You have to admit that your new facility is the talk of the town right now."

"I could have continued running my company from Virginia."

"It was time for you to come home, Ethan. You and I both know it. You have a lot of unfinished business here."

"We'll see."

Chandler laid down his menu. "Is your house going to be ready on time?"

Ethan nodded.

"What do you think of the office space?" Chandler asked. "The moment I saw the property listed, I felt like it was perfect for you."

Ethan chuckled. "You know me well. The building is perfect. I did find it interesting that my office is so close to the DuGrandpre location."

Chandler did not respond, but also did not bother to hide his amusement. "Have you spoken with Jordin yet?"

"As a matter of fact, she came to see me at my office last week," Ethan said. "You didn't have anything to do with that little meeting, did you? How did Jordin know where my office was located in the first place?"

Shrugging, Chandler responded, "I haven't spoken to Jordin in months."

"How about Ryker?"

Chandler grinned. "Well, I did run into him and his wife one evening."

"And you told Ryker I was back, right? I knew that Jordin and I would eventually run into one another but I didn't think it would be so soon. I wasn't prepared."

"Sounds like fate intervened."

Ethan shook his head no. "Not in the way you're thinking, Chandler. I can't deny that it was good to see her, but things are different between us now."

"In what way?"

"In every way that matters," Ethan stated. "Truth is that she's always been out of my league. I was just too stupid to realize it back then. No matter how much money I have, I will never be good enough for Etienne DuGrandpre's daughter. Her father tolerated our friendship, but I got the feeling that he did not want our relationship going further than that."

"That may have been true back then, Ethan," Chandler responded. "Jordin's old enough to make her own decisions. I don't think you should give up on her so easily. I know how much you care for her."

Ethan shrugged in nonchalance. "Her father never cared much for me though. Anyway, I've got too much baggage, Chandler."

"I don't think she'd allow her parents to pick her husband. Jordin's much too independent for that."

"I don't know…" Ethan uttered. He scanned his menu, trying to decide on what he wanted to eat.

His mind traveled back to Jordin. One of the qualities that attracted Ethan to Jordin was her genuine smile, which seemed prominently on display at all times. Her once shoulder-length hair was in a short bob. She wore no makeup outside of lipstick. Still, he found her incredibly sexy.

"How was your weekend with the girls?" Jadin inquired on Monday morning. "I couldn't come by because Michael and I had a serious conversation about our relationship."

"We had such a great time," Jordin responded as she prepared a cup of hot tea. "Kai and Amya missed you though."

Jadin poured coffee into a black mug. "I'll have to see if I can set up a movie date with them or something."

"I'm sure they would love it."

Jordin picked up a plate containing fresh fruit and a bagel. "The more time I spend with those little girls, the more I want to have children of my own. I can't wait to be a mother."

"You'd definitely be good at it," her sister responded.

She studied her sister's face. There was a hint of sadness behind Jadin's eyes. "Are you okay?"

"I'm fine."

"I know you, sis," Jordin stated. "You mentioned that you and Michael talked—is everything good between you two?"

"He's been offered a job with a large law firm in Beverly Hills."

She met her sister's gaze. "Is he going to take it?"

Jadin nodded. "He wants me to go with him."

"What did you say?" Jordin couldn't imagine her sister being thousands of miles away from her, but she would never try to stand in the way of Jadin's happiness.

"I told him that I couldn't. I could never do that to Dad. He's always drilled the importance of the DuGrand-pre legacy."

"Dad also wants you to be happy, Jadin. I'm sure he would understand."

"I'm not moving to California," she stated. "Michael understands my reasons why and while he isn't fond of the choice I made—he understands why I can't go."

"Yet you seem somewhat sad."

"I love Michael and I'm really going to miss him."

"Well, at least you can visit him."

She shook her head sadly. "I told him that I thought it was best to just be friends. I don't want Michael to feel obligated in trying to maintain a long-distance relationship."

"You just said that you love Michael," Jordin stated. "Why would you break up with him?" Deep down, she was thrilled because she suspected he was nothing more than a ladies' man. Jadin wanted to get married, but he always used the excuse that he wasn't ready.

"It's for the best, sis."

"For you or him?"

Jadin met her sister's gaze. "For both of us. We are DuGrandpres, Jordin. Our grandfather started this company from the ground up here in Charleston. I am proud of our duty to make sure his legacy is carried on. You remember how upset Granddad and Uncle Jacques got when Aubrie decided to become a chef?"

"Her father eventually accepted her decision," Jordin pointed out. "Granddad is still not happy about it though."

"Deep down, Uncle Jacques is not completely okay with it either."

She had to agree. It really hurt her uncle when his only daughter chose not to follow in her family's footsteps. Jordin glimpsed the longing in her sister's eyes. She knew that as much as Jadin wanted to be with Michael, she would never choose him over her family.

Despite her mixed feelings where Michael was concerned, Jordin did not necessarily agree with Jadin's unwavering loyalty to the family. It was time for her sister to selfishly consider her future with the man she loved. "Think of your own happiness for once."

"I always thought that you didn't care much for Michael," Jadin stated, "yet you are telling me to follow him to California."

"I don't believe he's the man for you," Jordin explained. "However, it is not my right to stand in the way of your happily-ever-after."

Jadin met her gaze. "I suppose you would like for me to do the same where you're concerned. Right?"

"What are you talking about?"

"Ethan."

"This isn't about me or Ethan, Jadin. We are talking about you and Michael."

"So if Ethan wanted you to leave the firm—would you?"

"I would consider his request," Jordin confessed.

"You would put a man before the good of our company… our family legacy?" Jadin questioned. A look of disbelief crossed her face.

"Our legacy is woven into the fabric of this beautiful city, sis. I am a DuGrandpre by blood and nothing will ever change this," Jordin stated. "However, I also deserve to be with someone who loves me. I want to create a legacy with my husband for our children. I would think that you'd have the same desires."

"The DuGrandpre name is a burden we have to bear, Jordin. We can't take it lightly."

"You sound like Granddad," she uttered in response.

"Granddad told us how he was threatened by a group of racists when he started the law firm. The original office was burned to the ground, but our grandfather didn't give up. Our company was founded on his blood, sweat and tears, Jordin."

"I know all of this, sis. I wouldn't do anything to tarnish our history, but I have the right to live my life on my own terms—we all have that right, Jadin."

"I'm afraid we are never going to agree on this subject," she responded with a sigh.

"Jadin, I don't disagree with you. I just believe that I can have a life of my own without bringing dishonor to my family. Aubrie has a very successful restaurant—this is an extension of the DuGrandpre legacy and there's nothing wrong with it. Our legacy reaches far beyond the law firm."

Her sister remained silent.

"I know you are beyond loyal, Jadin, and it's a wonderful quality. I am also loyal to this family and our company, but I am not going to give up on marriage and a family," Jordin stated. "No one requires this of us."

"I disagree."

"Well, I intend on living my life on my own terms, Jadin, and I suggest you do the same. If you don't…you may one day regret it."

Chapter 4

"Jordin, what are you doing here?" Ethan asked, surprised that she had come to the office to see him a second time.

She lifted her chin, ran her fingers through her hair as she walked toward him—she was electrifying. Her hair, her eyes, and the way her hips swayed invitingly when she walked, screamed sexy.

The soft tap of her heels against the marble floor sounded a steady rhythm, even over the noise of the employees scurrying around in the office. She did not stop until she was right in front of him. "I came to see you, silly."

"Let's talk in my office," he said.

The two walked in silence down the hallway.

Inside his office, Jordin's eyes traveled around the room. He had added more furnishings since the first time she visited. "Very nice…"

"It still needs a decorator's touch."

Her perfume reached for him, flavoring the air he breathed. Ethan looked down into her eyes, saw the sparkle and knew he was in deep trouble.

"Why don't you give my mother a call?" Jordin suggested. "I'm sure she'd welcome the opportunity to enter a bid to land the contract."

"She doesn't have to bid—I'll give her a call to see if she can schedule me in."

"I'm sure you'll be pleased with her work."

"I don't doubt that," he responded.

"I hope I'm not keeping you from anything," Jordin stated as she made herself comfortable in one of the visitor chairs.

"I always have time for my friends." He had a mild, interested tone.

"Really?" she asked. "I figured you must have been really busy since I haven't heard from you. We are still friends, right?"

"I deserve that."

"Yes you certainly do," Jordin responded. "I mean… not one phone call or text to just say a quick hello."

"I accept full responsibility for my actions. I have been busy too."

She sat with her arms folded across her chest.

"How can I make this up to you?"

"Why don't you come by my house for dinner this evening? I actually learned how to cook, although it was only out of necessity."

Ethan laughed. "Tell the truth…are the meals you prepare edible?"

"Yes, they are. I'm a really good cook. I learned from Aubrie."

"How is she doing?" he asked. "Chandler was crazy

about her, but she would never give him a second look, probably because he was Ryker's friend."

Jordin nodded in agreement. "She never wanted to be involved with any of her brother's friends. Aubrie has her own restaurant now."

"That's great. I can't believe there's actually a Du-Grandpre who did not go into law."

Jordin chuckled. "Both my grandfather and uncle went into shock when she told them she wanted to be a chef."

They were quiet for a few minutes.

"I really thought I would've heard from you," she blurted. "Since I haven't, I decided to come here so you can tell me why?"

"I know that I haven't been a very good friend."

"That's not at all what I'm saying, Ethan."

"It is what it is," he responded. "I didn't stay in contact with you as promised and now that I'm back…nothing has changed. I know this is what you're thinking."

"The thought crossed my mind once or twice."

"Let me make it up to you, Jordin. I ordered lunch for the staff," Ethan announced. "Do you have time to have to eat something? I want to continue our conversation about your so-called cooking skills. I have to confess that I'm not buying it. As I recall, you couldn't even make a decent mud pie when we were younger."

She laughed. "Yes, I can stay for lunch. As for the mud pie, I didn't like getting my hands dirty. Really, I can cook."

"I'll be the judge of that tonight."

Jordin broke into a huge grin. "So you're accepting my invitation, then?"

Ethan nodded. "We have a lot to talk about and I'd rather not do it here at the office."

"I understand," she murmured.

Ethan leaned back in the black leather desk chair, watching her.

Jordin's cell phone began to ring. She gave him an apologetic smile, and then said, "I need to take this call."

"Do you need some privacy? You can use the office across the hall."

"Thank you." She rose to her feet fluidly and headed to the door, saying, "I'll be right back."

She returned ten minutes later. "Sorry about that. I'm afraid I'm going to have to take a rain check on lunch, but I look forward to seeing you tonight. I'll text you my address."

"I'll make sure to bring my cast-iron stomach."

Jordin broke into a grin. "You are going to regret those words, Ethan Holbrooke."

He laughed as he escorted her out to the lobby area.

When he returned to his office, Ethan's eyes landed on the clock. He found himself looking forward to the evening. Spending time with Jordin filled him with an unexpected excitement.

The thought occurred to him that he never once considered turning down her invitation. He no longer wanted to keep his distance, an invisible string pulling him toward her. He longed to be in Jordin's presence, to hear her joyous laughter and her teasing.

"I'm cooking dinner for Ethan tonight," Jordin announced as she strolled into her sister's office later that afternoon.

Jadin's eyebrows rose in surprise. "*Really?* When did this happen?"

"A little more than an hour ago," she responded. "I went over to his office and invited him."

Her sister sighed in frustration. "Why are you doing

this to yourself? You gave Ethan your number which he never bothered to use, Jordin. I find that very telling."

"I didn't call him either."

"I know how badly you want to reconnect with him, but maybe you should sit back and wait for him to make a move."

"Jadin, I'm not going to play games," Jordin stated. "I care about Ethan and I miss our friendship—it's not about who makes the first move. I still consider him my best friend and I intend to make sure he knows it."

Her sister shrugged in nonchalance. "I don't know why I bother trying to discuss this with you. It's not like you ever listen to me."

"Sis, I hear what you're saying," Jordin responded. "But it doesn't change my feelings. I will always care for Ethan." She sighed softly. "Why can't you just be supportive?"

"Because it's not like you really know this man. I would feel differently if you two had been in touch all of these years."

"Jadin, the truth is that you never thought he was good enough for me—even when we were younger. I know that Dad felt the same way." Shaking her head, Jordin uttered, "I don't care what you all think where Ethan is concerned. I am not going to give up on him."

Ethan steered his SUV out of the parking lot and onto the street, per the vocal instructions of his GPS. He was not familiar with the area where she lived. He was mildly surprised that she did not live in the same Sullivan's Island neighborhood where her parents and Ryker lived.

He arrived at her condominium located in the Village at Wild Dunes almost thirty minutes later.

The Isle of Palms area drew thousands of tourists annually. Jordin loved the beach, so he was not surprised she would choose a waterfront residence.

Ethan parked his car, climbed out and walked up to the front door with a bouquet of yellow roses for Jordin.

When Ethan entered the residence, the delicious scent of freshly sautéed garlic and herbs assaulted him.

His eyes landed on Jordin, who was wearing a clingy black dress that landed right above her knees and a pair of sexy high-heeled sandals. "You look beautiful," Ethan murmured.

"Thank you," she responded with a smile. "Now that we've got that out of the way, I'm going to change really quickly into a pair of comfortable jeans and shoes. I hope you don't mind."

Ethan burst into laughter. "There's the girl I remember."

"I would keep this on, but my shoes are killing me."

"You can just take your shoes off," he suggested.

"Naaah… I wanted to impress you. Now I just want to be comfortable."

"I was greatly impressed," Ethan confirmed.

"Good. Now I can get comfortable." She tossed him the TV remote. "Find something interesting to watch."

Ethan's gaze traveled his surroundings. The mustard-colored walls and deep-purple-colored drapes provided a richly colorful backdrop while soft music floated throughout the house. Jordin had wonderful views of palm trees, lush landscaping and the beach.

She chose contemporary furnishings to decorate the spacious floor plan. The dining area was large enough for a table of six and overflowed into the great room. He liked the purple-and-gold theme accented with sage-green accessories.

"Did your mother decorate this place?" Ethan asked her when she returned to the living room.

Jordin shook her head. "No, I insisted on doing it on my own. She did make some suggestions, however."

"You have a nice home."

"Thanks. Have you found someplace to live?"

He nodded. "Yes, I'll be moving in a couple of weeks. Remember the house we used to dream of living in on Orange Street?"

She met his gaze. "No way... You bought it?"

He nodded. "I did."

"I loved that house," Jordin murmured. "I used to imagine us sitting out on the terrace drinking lemonade and talking about everything under the sun. I love the double piazzas."

"You have to see the inside of the house," Ethan said. "Multiple French doors, high ceilings and hardwood floors throughout."

"How many bedrooms do you have?" she asked. "I'm sure it has to be four or five."

"Actually, I have six bedrooms and five baths. There is also a two-story guest cottage in the back with two bedrooms."

"I told you there was another place in the back, re-member?"

Ethan smiled. "You were right."

"I hope you'll give me a tour of the house. I've wanted to see inside for so many years... I can't believe you bought our place." Jordin gave a short laugh. "I guess it's just your place now."

"When I found that it was for sale—I felt like it was a sign that I should buy it."

"I'm so glad you did, Ethan." Jordin said with a smile. Their gazes met and held.

"Okay, so why don't we address the elephant in the room?"

He chuckled. "Same Jordin. You won't give up until you have all of the answers."

"That's because you've always done a pretty good job of keeping secrets. I just thought that we had gotten way beyond that."

"I wasn't trying to keep secrets from you, Jordin. I just didn't want you knowing just how terrible things were for me at home."

"Ethan, that's what I don't get," she murmured. "Why not? We were best friends. I used to tell you everything."

"You are a DuGrandpre. I didn't think you could understand what I was dealing with."

"My family isn't perfect, Ethan."

"They were as near perfect as I could imagine." Ethan paused a few seconds before continuing. "I'm sure you heard rumors about my mother."

"Not really," she responded. "I only heard that she abandoned you and that's why you had to go live with your father."

"My mom and Rob went to Maryland with a trunk full of drugs. They were stopped by the police and arrested."

Jordin gasped in surprise. "Are you serious?"

He nodded. Lydia went to prison. That's where she's been until recently."

"She's out now?"

"Yeah," he grunted in response. "Talk about bad timing. She was released around the same time I moved back to Charleston."

Jordin could hardly believe what she was hearing. "I had no idea."

"I never wanted you to know," Ethan admitted.

She reached out, taking his hand into her own. "You

have no reason to be ashamed. None of this was of your doing."

He shrugged in nonchalance. "My mother completely changed when she met Rob. She only thought of her own happiness."

"If you'd told me, I know that my parents would've helped—even taken you in, Ethan. You didn't have to go through this alone."

"Chandler told me the same thing. I know his parents offered to be my foster parents but my father claimed he wanted me to live with him. I spent two weeks with him before he sent me to Hargrave Military Academy."

Jordin rose to her feet. "Dinner's ready. Why don't we continue our conversation in the dining room?"

"I've been anticipating this all day." He stood up.

She laughed. "Don't you really mean dreading?"

He chuckled and realized that he'd missed this too. The verbal sparring between them.

"What do you think?" Jordin asked after he tried his chicken.

Ethan wiped his mouth on his napkin. "This is delicious. Tell the truth. You didn't really cook this meal."

"Yeah, I did." Jordin broke into a grin. "I told you that I had some skills."

"You also have a cousin who owns her own restaurant," Ethan pointed out.

Stiffening, she folded her arms across her chest. "So what are you trying to say? I don't fake my meals for any man."

"I'm only teasing you," Ethan confessed. He laughed at the expression on her face.

Jordin relaxed and settled back against her chair.

"So tell me, is there someone special in your life?" he inquired while slicing up his meat.

Jordin shook her head no. "My job keeps me pretty busy."

Ethan wiped his mouth with the edge of his napkin. "You sound like me."

"Some would call us workaholics, although I do take time to enjoy life," Jordin stated. "I guess I play as hard as I work. How about you?"

"I'm probably every aspect of a classic workaholic," he responded candidly. "I take little time out to just relax. Right now, I need to focus on work though. By the end of the year, I plan to go somewhere tropical and relaxing."

"But in the meantime, you surround yourself with tropical artwork." She could still recall the paintings displayed around his office.

He nodded. "I want my employees to feel relaxed while working."

Jordin met Ethan's gaze with a smile. "I'm really glad you decided to accept my dinner invitation. It's great being able to spend time with you again."

Ethan took a long sip of his iced tea before responding, "I'm glad I came. Even though I didn't stay in contact, I want you to know that you were really missed." His gaze traveled over her face and searched her eyes.

"When I never heard from you, I just assumed that you were either abducted by aliens or that there were no phones in North Carolina or Virginia." Jordin paused a moment before adding, "I guess they didn't have any computers either."

Ethan fixed his gaze on hers and responded, "Jordin, it was nothing like that at all."

"Then what was it? Why didn't I hear from you? I checked my mailbox for a year, looking for a letter from you."

"Jordin, I didn't know what to say about my situation. I was angry and apprehensive about living with a man I didn't really know. When he sent me away, I used my anger to fuel my motivation to become the man that I am today."

"And since you've been back? I've basically had to chase you down."

"I…" He could not think of a plausible excuse. How could he tell Jordin that the pull of her was inexorable? What man in his right mind wouldn't be fascinated by her? Ethan cut off his straying thoughts.

"I guess it doesn't really matter anymore," Jordin stated. "You're here now and I hope from this moment forward—we can be friends again."

"We will always be friends," Ethan responded. "I apologize for the way I've behaved. I wanted to talk to you, but I let other stuff get in the way. I saw you and Jadin one afternoon having lunch at the deli on the corner. I considered joining you…"

"Why didn't you?"

"I know your sister doesn't care much for me."

"It doesn't matter what Jadin thinks," Jordin stated. "You should have come inside the deli. Tell me something, Ethan. How many girls have you picked up from one of your gyms? Be honest."

He laughed. "None."

"You want me to believe that you've never picked up a girl at the gym? Not even once?"

"Not even once," Ethan repeated. "My turn. Have you dated any of the firm's clientele?"

Jordin shook her head no. "I consider it a conflict of interest."

"Same here," he responded. "I've had some women show interest in me, but I just don't go there with them."

"Have you been serious with anyone?"

Ethan took a long sip of iced tea. "Not really. You?"

"No. My focus has been on being a good lawyer. It's the DuGrandpre way." She paused a heartbeat before saying, "We actually have had a new family member come on board. My brother, Austin."

"Really? I thought you all never had any contact with him."

"We didn't until recently. He is a lawyer and he moved here to work with Dad."

"How do you feel about it?" Ethan inquired.

"I'm okay with it," Jordin answered. "I don't have any evidence to suspect otherwise, but I do think there's another reason he's here. He's good at his job though."

"Why do you think he has another reason than getting to know his family? Is it because he's an outsider?"

"No, nothing like that, Ethan," she said, sensing a change in his mood. "We have always wanted to have Austin in our lives. It was his mother who kept him away from us."

"I know how it feels to be an outsider in your own family."

"Austin is my brother and I'm thrilled to finally have the chance to get to know him. I just hope he doesn't have a secret agenda because I don't want my father to get hurt."

Wiping her mouth with the corner of her napkin, Jordin stated, "Enough about Austin. I want to talk about us."

"Okay."

"Ethan, it's very clear to me that if I hadn't run into you earlier—I wouldn't be having dinner with you now."

"You're probably right," Ethan admitted after a moment. "But maybe not."

Jordin let her fork drop from her fingers. "What do you mean by that exactly?"

"A couple of times I did consider contacting you while I was in Virginia," Ethan confessed. "But in the end, I didn't call."

"Why not? If you really cared about our friendship." Jordin asked as she reached for her water glass. She took one sip, then another. And another.

"Jordin, it's not what you're thinking."

Instead of meeting his gaze, she pushed her broccoli from one side to the other with her fork. "We were close, Ethan. At least I thought we were."

"We are friends, Jordin," he stated. "I should have contacted you all those years ago, and because I didn't… well…I didn't feel right doing so now. The truth is that I don't deserve your friendship after the way I behaved."

Jordin shrugged in nonchalance. "I don't think you should spend too much time dwelling on past mistakes, Ethan. Life is way too short."

"Does this mean I get a do-over?"

Biting down on her lower lip, Jordin uttered, "Something like that."

Ethan reached out, lacing his fingers with her own. "Jordin, I can't tell you how glad I am to have you back in my life." His hand was strong, firm and protective.

"I will always be here for you, Ethan. I want you to know this."

He pulled his hand away from her, his lips puckered in annoyance. "Jordin, let's be clear. I don't need your pity."

"I don't pity you, Ethan. I just figured you might need a good friend." She finished off the last of her chicken. Shrugging, Jordin added, "I made the offer—it's up to you to accept."

He wiped his mouth on the edge of his napkin. "I apologize."

"I don't need your apology, Ethan. What I do need from you is honesty. If you don't want my friendship any longer...just tell me."

"I see," he murmured. "You're still as feisty as I remembered."

"I don't see any need to change, Ethan."

He broke into a smile. "I'm inclined to agree with you." Ethan laid down his fork. "You are one of my closest friends, Jordin. It's just that back then, I could see the pity on people's faces...it tore me up inside. I only considered coming back to Charleston when I knew I was ready."

"Why do you care what others think?"

"I really don't," he responded.

"So your reason for not contacting me was that you thought I would pity you."

"Can you honestly say otherwise?" Ethan questioned. "I saw how you reacted every time you heard about someone being mistreated."

"I don't pity you. I just feel bad because you didn't deserve what happened to you."

"I know that none of this was my fault." Ethan wiped his mouth on the end of his napkin. "If you don't mind, I'd rather not talk about this anymore."

They finished off the rest of their meal in silence.

When they were done, he helped her clean the kitchen.

"Are you still an art lover?" Ethan asked while putting a plate into the dishwasher.

When Jordin nodded, he said, "I was invited to a gallery opening. Would you like to be my date?"

Jordin turned to look at him. "Really?"

"Yeah. I don't want to attend the event alone."

"Sure, I'd love to attend."

"It's on Saturday at seven. I'll call you to finalize the details before the end of the week."

Folding her arms across her chest, she stated, "I'm warning you now, Ethan. Don't stand me up."

"I'm not that bad, Jordin."

She met his gaze and said, "You'd better not do something like that to me."

There was a tingling in the pit of his stomach. "I give you my word that I'll be there."

Ethan had to fight his overwhelming need to be close to her, reminding him why he'd stayed away from Jordin since his return—it was better than facing what she meant to him. Even standing in the kitchen so close to her was torturous. He purposely avoided looking at her mouth, seeking to ignore how Jordin's full, luscious lips beckoned to him.

His dark eyes were framed by his handsome face while his lips parted and showed a dazzling display of straight, white teeth. His profile was proud and full of strength, a quality that could be attributed to his commanding presence.

Their gazes met and held, making Jordin nervous. She thought she detected a flicker in his intense eyes, causing her pulse to skitter alarmingly. Jordin never tired of looking at him.

Ethan followed her into the family room where they settled on the sofa.

"We'll have to do this again sometime," Ethan stated. "Only next time, I'll show off my culinary skills"

"Sure," she replied with complacent buoyancy. "This I can't wait to see."

He laughed.

"You in a kitchen cooking—I will definitely have to witness this for myself."

"Hey, I had to learn how to cook out of my need to survive."

Jordin smiled. "This feels almost like a dream. Sitting here with you…"

"This is for real," Ethan assured her. "I'm back."

"I guess you're here to stay since you relocated your office and purchased a home in Charleston. I'm really happy about that."

He picked up a magazine off her table. "You still read these?"

Jordin nodded. "I have to keep up with the latest fashions."

"Bedazzled anything lately?"

Laughing, she gave him a soft punch in the arm. "I was a trendsetter."

Jordin was having the time of her life with Ethan. Happiness filled her as they talked and laughed about old times until well after midnight.

She stifled a yawn. "This is wonderful."

"I've had a great time but I can tell you're tired. You're fighting to keep your eyes open."

"I'm sorry." She really wasn't ready for the evening to come to an end.

"Don't apologize, Jordin," Ethan responded. "I'm going to make my way back to my hotel so I can fall into bed myself. It's been a long day."

She rose to her feet and embraced him. "I have probably said this a million times—I'm glad to see you."

Ethan had no idea that his return was a dream come true for Jordin.

Chapter 5

Why did I just ask her out? Ethan wanted to take the words back as soon as they came out of his mouth, but it was already too late. It was taking every effort he could draw on to keep up his guard. Jordin still affected him in so many ways.

Instead of going back to the hotel, Ethan went to his office, hoping to work off some of the tension. When he left Jordin's house, he felt as if every nerve in his body was on alert.

The telephone rang.

He picked it up without thinking. "Hello."

Silence.

"Hello," he repeated.

Ethan waited for a response. When there was none forthcoming, he hung up.

The phone rang again.

He did not recognize the number on the caller ID. The

office was closed, so who could be calling at this late hour? he wondered.

Curiosity got the best of him, prompting him to pick up the receiver. "Hello."

"Ethan, it's me. I've been trying to reach you. I took a chance that you would be working late."

His mouth took on an unpleasant twist. "We have nothing to talk about, Lydia."

"Son, please give me a chance to explain."

"Explain what?" he snapped in anger. "That you went to prison for trafficking drugs with your boyfriend. It's self-explanatory."

"It's not like that, Ethan."

He did not respond.

His mouth thinned with displeasure. "Goodbye, Lydia."

"Please..." his mother pleaded on the other end of the phone line. "Please don't hang up on me. I—"

He cut her off by interjecting, "Do me a favor and never call me ever again. I don't need a mother now."

"You have no idea what I had to go through to find you when I got out of prison. Your father wouldn't tell me where you were. I missed you so much, Ethan."

"You needn't have bothered looking for me," he replied; his face felt tight with strain. "Just leave me alone."

Ethan hung up.

Although he hated to admit it, even to himself, the call had unnerved him.

An image of Jordin appeared in his mind. His thoughts of her infectious smile warmed him all over. Ethan took a deep breath and exhaled, adjusting his mood.

Long after Ethan had left, she was still up.

Jordin was tired, but had trouble falling asleep. Humming softly to the music, she turned on her laptop. She had really enjoyed his visit. Seeing Ethan again brought back feelings that she had buried a long time ago.

Jordin was physically attracted to Ethan, but that attraction ran more than skin-deep. She had always believed their relationship was a special one and what she felt for him defied definition.

It was one of the reasons she couldn't fully understand why he had a huge wall between them. Jadin was right about him being distant and very guarded. Jordin assumed it was a result of his past experiences, but they had been close. Surely, Ethan knew that he could trust her.

Jordin glanced over at the clock, and then pushed her puzzling thoughts aside because she needed to shift into work mode.

An hour later, Jordin was still reviewing case files when the telephone rang.

"Hello," she murmured into the receiver.

"I know it's late, but I wanted to wait until I thought Ethan was gone. How did everything go?"

"It was great, Jadin. Ethan and I did some catching up and he invited me to an art gallery opening this Saturday."

"It sounds like you two didn't have any problems reconnecting."

"We didn't."

"I'm glad to hear it," her sister stated. "I'm going to bed and we can talk tomorrow. Aubrie dropped off some of her banana nut muffins, so I'll bring you some."

"Great. Good night, sis." Jordin hung up and returned her attention to the documents spread out on her bed. It was after two in the morning. She put everything away and turned off the lights.

* * *

Two days later, Jordin moved around her bedroom in a panic. "Why on earth did I agree to go to this opening tonight? I have no idea what to wear."

Jordin called her sister. "I really need your help. I'm not sure what I should wear for this event."

"What about that outfit I bought you for your birthday last year? I'm sure it's hanging in the closet with the tags still on it."

"I think it's much too sexy for a gallery opening, Jadin."

"Isn't that the idea?"

Jordin laughed. "No, it's not."

"Okay, so what time is your date?"

Jordin glanced over at the clock. "In a couple of hours."

"I'll be there in about ten minutes."

"Thanks," Jordin said, her voice filled with relief. "I appreciate your help."

She hung up the phone and sat down to wait for her sister to arrive.

"Help has arrived," Jadin announced, walking briskly through the door. "I can't believe you're acting so nervous. It's just Ethan."

Jordin led her to the bedroom.

Inside, she pointed to the peach-colored dress on the bed. "I was thinking about wearing this but it looks kind of boring, don't you think?"

"Well, it's not what I would wear."

"I was going to pair it with a pair of turquoise pumps."

Jadin smiled. "I like it."

She gave her sister a glance. "Really?"

"I think it's perfect. Jordin, you don't need a stylist. What's up? I've never seen you this way."

"I want to make a great impression on Ethan. He probably remembers me as the teen who wore nothing but jeans…"

"And your obsession with the Bedazzler machine," Jadin finished for her.

"Hey, everybody wanted jeans like mine."

They both laughed.

"Seriously, I really want to look nice for Ethan."

"Jordin, you will knock his socks off with this outfit. Are you planning on wearing any makeup?"

Jordin frowned. "Do I need to?"

"Just a little," Jadin suggested. "Just to enhance your natural beauty."

After she was dressed, her sister broke into a smile. "You look gorgeous, sis."

Jordin dismissed her words with a wave of her hand. "Be serious."

"I am," she responded.

Jadin left within minutes of Ethan's scheduled arrival.

Jordin surveyed her reflection in the mirror once more, pleased with what she saw.

"You look beautiful," he complimented when she opened the door to let him enter the house.

"Thanks," she said with a smile.

Jordin grabbed her purse. "I'm ready."

"Great," Ethan murmured. "Let's go appreciate some art."

She laughed. "Why do we always end up going to art galleries and museums when you don't like doing stuff like this?"

"I know you like it," he responded. "Your mother used to always take us to gallery openings and artist show-cases."

Jordin nodded in agreement. "She always said it was so that we would develop an appreciation for art."

"She is the reason I am an art lover and collector."

"I love the pieces you selected for your office. I would have imagined that you preferred abstract art over the landscape scenes."

"I chose those pieces for a reason," Ethan explained as he drove toward downtown Charleston. "Research studies have shown that vivid paintings of landscapes can lower blood pressure and heart rate, while abstract pictures can have the opposite effect. I chose waterfalls and beachfront scenes to inspire a sense of peace in the workplace. It's important that my employees feel energized and motivated throughout the day to complete their duties."

"Wow, I'm impressed."

Ethan smiled. "Like I said, I have your mother to thank for introducing me to the beauty of art."

"She is going to be thrilled to hear this. None of her own children have such a strong affection for art."

Chapter 6

"Have you eaten here before?" Ethan asked after they left the art gallery.

Jordin nodded. "I've only been here a couple of times. The food is really great. A whole lot better than those edible art displays they served at that art gallery. I couldn't recognize any of the food."

He laughed. "Who knew you could make appetizers look so unique and unrecognizable?"

"I know. I did hear someone say that the owner is vegan, so that's probably why we didn't know what we were eating. Some of it wasn't bad though. They were beautiful to look at—like miniature pieces of artwork."

He was in awe of the way Jordin looked at the world through eyes that searched out and found beauty in the most unlikely places. "You're still more adventurous than I am," Ethan stated. "I refuse to eat something that I have no idea of the ingredients."

They were seated immediately.

Shortly after, a waiter arrived to take their drink orders.

Ethan scanned the menu. "Any recommendations?"

"You really can't go wrong with anything."

"If the food here is so great, why have you only come a couple of times?" Ethan inquired.

She smiled. "I prefer Aubrie's restaurant."

Grinning, Ethan responded, "Imagine that. The Du-Grandpre family are known for their loyalty to one another."

Their eyes locked as their breathing seemed to come in unison.

Their waiter appeared once more with drinks and prepared to take their selections.

When he was gone, Jordin questioned,

"Why did you say that?"

"Because it's true," he responded. "It's not a criticism, Jordin."

"It sounds like one."

"It's one of the qualities I do admire about your family," Ethan stated. "You all love each other and will do whatever is necessary to protect one another."

"You know I actually saw a few pieces that I really liked at the gallery," Jordin stated, wanting to change the subject.

"So did I," he responded. "I noticed you have some nice artwork on your walls."

"I've picked up a few pieces here and there. My mom's the serious art collector. You should see her collection." Jordin's eyes traveled the length of the restaurant. "I'm glad we did this."

Ethan met her gaze. "Why is that?"

"Because it reminds me of how we were when we

were younger. We had so many dreams and places we
wanted to go."

Memories raced through his mind, causing sensory
overload. He remembered the arguments, the conversations and the feelings of rejection… "Then real life happened," he uttered.

Jordin met his gaze. "Ethan, please."

"*What?* Don't sound so bitter?" He paused for a few
seconds before adding, "I'm sorry, but I don't really have
fond memories of my youth."

"Not even of the time we spent together?"

Ethan did not respond.

The waiter's appearance put a temporary hold on their
conversation. He placed their entrees on the table.

Ethan said a quick blessing over the food.

Jordin took a bite and closed her eyes, savoring the
flavor. "This is so good."

She looked at him. "What's wrong?" she asked, point-
ing to his plate. "Aren't you hungry?"

His gaze was on her and Jordin tried to throttle the
dizzying current racing through her body. "You're staring," Jordin murmured. She wished for a moment that
she could hide from the intensity in his eyes.

"You have grown into an incredibly beautiful woman."

"Thank you for the compliment," she said. "You're
very sweet."

He had complimented her at least twice on her dress
and her hair. Jordin noted how handsome Ethan looked
in the gray suit he was wearing. Each time she saw him,
the pull was stronger.

Jordin picked up her glass of wine, took a long sip and
then set it down again. "This was a great choice in restaurants." She used the corner of her napkin to wipe her
mouth. "Have you ever been here before?"

Shaking his head, Ethan responded, "This is my first time."

"How did you know about Bastile? It's only been in Charleston for almost a year."

"I asked Walter for a recommendation. He also suggested your cousin's restaurant."

She gave him a sidelong glance. "Ethan, can I ask you a question?"

He met her gaze. "Sure."

"Do you ever just relax?" she asked.

Stroking his chin, Ethan regarded her carefully. "Not really, but believe it or not—I actually know how to have a good time."

"What constitutes a good time to you?" Jordin questioned with a grin. "What is it that you do for fun?"

Ethan leaned forward, gazing into her eyes. "Do you really want to know what I enjoy doing for pleasure?"

Jordin flushed hotly as her gaze snapped to his.

Ethan broke into laughter at the expression on her face. "I enjoy reading mysteries. Going to art museums, exhibits…stuff like that. I do it because it reminded me of you."

"Oh…"

"So what do you do for fun these days?" he inquired, a soft smile curving his mouth.

"I'm sure you remember how much I love the water. I still spend a lot of time on the beach during the summer," Jordin responded. "I'm also a huge history buff— I'm always taking tours and of course, I still love music."

"Interesting… I love history myself," Ethan commented.

The warmth of his smile echoed in his voice.

"There are a couple of contemporary art exhibits in Charleston but they're only going to be here for a couple of weeks," Jordin announced. "Would you like to see them?"

Ethan held her gaze. "I'd love to," he responded, giving her a smile that sent her pulses racing. His eyes shimmered with the light from the window.

After their dinner, neither one of them wanted to end the evening, so they went back to her place after leaving the restaurant. Jordin made a pot of coffee, and then sat down with Ethan in the living room.

"I'm glad to see that you're not as much of a stuffed shirt as I thought you were." She handed him a mug of coffee.

He chuckled. "I haven't changed that much, Jordin."

"I must have looked a hot mess when we were younger from the way you keep staring at me."

Ethan chuckled. "Not at all. It's taking me a minute to get used to you all grown-up."

"If you'd stayed in touch, we could have grown together."

"I thought you had forgiven me for that."

"I did," Jordin confirmed. "I'm just not going to let you forget it so easily."

"Same Jordin…" he murmured with a chuckle. "I have to remember to stay off your bad side."

She took a sip of her coffee as she studied him. Jordin couldn't deny the spark of excitement at the prospect of being with Ethan in a romantic relationship. Her emotions whirled. Blood pounded in her brain, leapt from her heart and made her knees tremble.

Ethan finished one cup of coffee before announcing, "I have an early day tomorrow, so I should get going."

Their gazes locked and she could see the attraction mirrored in his eyes.

Ethan pulled Jordin into his arms, surprising her.

He kissed her.

"Good night," he whispered.

For a brief moment, Ethan had let down his guard, allowing her a glimpse of affection. It was only a matter of time, Jordin decided.

Jordin had the ability to cut through his defenses and bring him to his knees. She had such a warm, loving spirit, and kept a permanent smile on her face.

He couldn't resist kissing her at least once. Ethan yearned to taste the sweetness of Jordin's lips and hold her close. He had been fantasizing about kissing her when the act became a reality, surprising them both.

Ethan had no regrets. The kiss was something that had haunted him since they were teens. However, he could not let his yearnings get out of control.

I have real feelings for this woman, and I can't see my life without her in it, but I have to be realistic. Nothing could ever become of his feelings for Jordin, so Ethan had no other choice—he had to accept that they could only be friends. Nothing more.

He changed clothes and climbed into bed.

Sleep eluded him, however. Ethan's head was filled with thoughts of Jordin.

He tossed from one side to the other, seeking out comfort.

Ethan gave up after an hour passed and he was no closer to sleep. He set up in bed, propping himself against his pillows.

Watching television was just as futile. Ethan stole a glance at the clock on his nightstand and groaned.

He had a very long day ahead of him.

Jordin's phone rang a few minutes after she entered her office. "Hey, sis," she said, recognizing the phone number.

"How was your date with Ethan?" Jadin asked. "Did he like your dress?"

"Ethan definitely liked my dress. We had a great time," she told her. Jordin decided to keep the kiss she and Ethan shared to herself.

"Have you told Mom and Dad that Ethan's back?"

"Mom knows because she's working on a project for him," Jordin stated. "I'm sure she's mentioned Ethan's return to Dad."

Her sister did not offer a response and she hadn't really expected one.

"Jadin, I don't expect you to understand my relationship with Ethan."

"I'm not going there, sis. I'm just glad you had a great evening."

"I really did." She was grateful that Jadin had decided to back off. They were close and she did not want anything coming between them.

They talked for a few minutes more before ending the call.

Jordin touched her lips as she recalled the kiss. It was sweet and gentle. She knew that Ethan would take things slow—it was the type of person he was and had always been. He was a good man. Together, they would make a great team.

But before anything could progress between them, she had to get Ethan to unlock his heart.

The rest of her day went by as smoothly as it had started. Jordin left the office and met up with an old classmate for drinks.

"Cheryl, I'm sorry I'm late. Traffic was backed up due to an accident."

"It's all good. I just got here about five minutes ago."

Jordin embraced her friend. "It's good to see you."

They sat down at a nearby table.

"What have you been up to?" Cheryl inquired.

"Work," she responded with a laugh. "How about you?"

"Same here. I have been in court most of this week." Shaking her head, Cheryl said, "Some days I question why I became a lawyer. On other days, I love my job."

"I understand," Jordin replied. "I feel the same way."

The waiter came to take their order.

He returned a few minutes later with two glasses of white wine.

Cheryl took a sip. "So are you dating anyone?"

Jordin shook her head. "No, I'm still very single."

"Any prospects?"

She smiled. "I have one."

"Tell me about him."

"Not yet," Jordin said. She picked up her glass and sipped her wine.

"This doesn't have anything to do with Mr. Ethan Holbrooke, does it?"

She was stunned. "Why would you ask that?"

Cheryl laughed. "When I first met you, Ethan was all you talked about. I figured since he was back in Charleston—you two would hook up."

"We haven't hooked up, but we have reconnected."

"Sounds like a love story in the making."

Smiling, Jordin took another sip. "I guess we'll have to see." She was trying not to set her hopes too high where Ethan was concerned.

"Well, he is a very handsome man," Cheryl stated. "The newspaper did an article on him."

"I'm so proud of him."

Cheryl finished off her wine and signaled for another.

"If he knew just how much you care for him—I'm sure he would have come back a lot sooner."

Jordin was not so assured.

He took hold of her shoulders, pulled her in close and kissed her. Jordin was leaning into him, kissing him as if that kiss meant life itself. Fiery darts of pleasure shot through him, enflaming his body. Her hands on his back seared through the shirt he was wearing.

Her gaze said what her mouth could not.

Ethan woke up from the dream that was quickly becoming erotic. This was not the first time he'd had dreams of this nature where Jordin was concerned. He turned from one side to the other, Jordin still heavy on his mind.

He had thoroughly enjoyed spending time with her earlier. For a moment, he was able to forget that so much time had passed between them. Jordin was still witty and she never did anything to try to impress him—she was comfortable in her own skin, a quality he admired.

Ethan and Jordin were longtime friends. He reminded himself that she cared for him like a brother and he did not want to cross the imaginary boundary lines.

He sat up in bed, propping himself up against the pillows.

Ethan felt the urge to call Jordin. He wanted to hear her voice, to have one of the long, late-night conversations like they did when they were younger.

Everything was different now. They were no longer teens. Ethan's life changed when he was forced to leave Charleston all those years ago. As much as he wanted to forget about the past, it was not easy because it was a large part of the man he had become.

Chapter 7

"Where were you last night?" Chandler inquired when Ethan joined him at a restaurant near his hotel. "I stopped by your place to see if you wanted to grab a bite to eat."

"Jordin and I attended a gallery opening," he responded. "She and I had dinner afterward."

Chandler broke into a grin. "That didn't take long."

"It was two old friends catching up—that's all," Ethan blurted.

"For now..."

"It's the way it will always be."

Frowning, Chandler inquired, "Why do you say that? Anybody that knows you knows that you're crazy about Jordin."

"For one thing, I don't have time for a relationship. The other is that I have too much baggage."

"This is your perception, but I don't think Jordin is

going to let you get away that easy. She really cares a lot about you."

"Jordin only sees me as a friend," Ethan stressed. "Nothing more."

Chandler shook his head. "For some reason, I don't believe that. I've seen the way she used to look at you."

"Do you know how long ago that was?" Ethan questioned. "We haven't seen each other in eleven years. A lot has changed."

"I'm not buying it, man. You need to get some glasses or something."

Ethan gave a short laugh. "You don't know what you're talking about."

"All right, man…"

The waiter came over to take their drink and food orders.

Ethan was glad for the minor interruption.

All around them, couples sat at small tables, leaning toward each other, laughing and talking. Waitstaff moved through the room serving up food and drinks.

"This place stays busy," Chandler stated.

The clink of glassware and waves of conversation drifted and hummed in the background.

Keeping his voice low in spite of the surrounding clatter, Ethan said, "I didn't intend on seeing Jordin until I felt I was ready. She came to me."

"Did you expect otherwise?"

He gave a slight nod. "I did, but I know Jordin, so I shouldn't have been surprised."

"You're a lucky man, Ethan. You have someone who truly cares for you, but you persist on being stubborn."

"I care for her as well," Ethan admitted. "But, Chandler, you know how her family can be—I have had enough family drama to last a lifetime. Not only that, I am focusing on building my company. I want gyms in every state. I have a lot of work ahead of me."

"So you're saying you have no time for love."

Ethan nodded. "That's it in a nutshell."

"I don't agree," Chandler stated. "If you wait too long, you're going to lose Jordin for good."

Ethan drew out of his pocket a folded stack of bills and peeled off two of them to toss onto the table. "I've got this."

Chandler's words echoed long after the two men parted.

Ethan kept hearing them over and over in his head. Now that Jordin was back in his life, he did not want to lose her.

Saturday evening, Jadin passed the bowl of popcorn to Jordin. "I know you and Ethan have been spending time together, but you're not getting your hopes up, are you?" She had come to Jordin's house to watch a movie.

Jordin rolled her eyes upward. "Not this again, Jadin. I'm not going to have this conversation with you."

"I'm sorry, but I care about you. I don't want you to get hurt by this man."

She eyed Jadin, asking, "Why are you so convinced that he's going to hurt me?"

"Because I know that you are in love with him. Can you say that he feels the same way about you?"

Her words stung Jordin. "It's not really your concern."

Sighing in resignation, Jadin uttered, "I see you're not going to listen to me."

"Not about this," Jordin responded. "Sis, remember how you didn't want to hear about my suspicions when it came to Michael? Well, I feel the same way when it comes to Ethan."

Her sister shook her head sadly.

"Jadin, I'm a grown woman. If Ethan doesn't have any interest in me—I can take the rejection. I believe you're wrong, however."

"I'll be around if you need me, Jordin."

"I know," she responded, "and I need you to have faith in me on this. You don't know Ethan like I do. Right now, he has trust issues, but the more time we spend together—the easier it will be for him to let down his guard."

"What exactly happened to him?"

"Apparently, the rumors about Rob being a drug dealer were true," Jordin stated. "Everyone assumed his mother just up and abandoned Ethan, but she ended up going to prison for transporting drugs with her boyfriend."

"That's a lot for a teen to handle."

Jordin agreed. "Then he was sent to live with his father, a man that didn't really want him around. He sent Ethan to a military academy in Virginia."

"So why didn't he try to contact us? Dad could've probably helped Ethan."

"I know. That's what I told him, but Ethan said he didn't want our pity. He's a very proud man, Jadin."

"I find that admirable."

"So do I," Jordin stated. "I just wish I could get him to see that. I have nothing but admiration for his courage and the man he has become."

"You have a lot of confidence in Ethan," Jadin commented. "It makes me question what I feel about Michael. I don't have that kind of confidence in him."

"Ethan and I have been friends a long time, even though we were apart all those years. It's different than the relationship you and Michael have."

"I suppose you're right."

Jordin looked at her sister. "What are you going to do about Michael? Are you really going to just end things?"

"I'm not moving to California, sis." Jadin took a sip of her soda. "I belong here."

She did not respond. Jordin did not agree with her sister, but decided that maybe it was for the best. If Jadin truly loved Michael—she would not think twice about leaving to be with him. If Ethan asked her to leave with him, Jordin would not hesitate because she knew that her future was with him. The fact that he did not seem to feel the same way bothered her deep down.

Jordin was not sure he even remembered those conversations, and she really did not expect him to do so, because they were only kids. Yet, she had carried those dreams with her—as she aged; her desire for the dream to become a reality grew with her.

"Austin, how are things going with you?" Jordin asked her brother the following Monday. They had just walked out of a meeting with her father. "Do you enjoy living in Charleston?"

"It's been good so far," he responded. "I'm sitting second chair on a case with Jadin at the end of the week."

"How are things with you and Dad?"

"We're getting to know one another."

Jordin didn't press for more information from Austin.

"I'll be at the house on Sunday for dinner," he blurted. "My first family dinner."

She broke into a smile. "We're celebrating your passing the South Carolina state bar exam."

"I didn't expect anyone to make a big deal out of it. It's not my first exam. I've been practicing law for a few years now."

"It's not just about the exam, Austin. We want to formally welcome you into the family."

"I wasn't sure how your mother would feel with me around."

"This was her idea to have this dinner for you," Jordin stated. "She's never had a problem with you. Mom has never had an issue with you or your mother."

Austin met her gaze. "I recognized a few years back that my mother is a bitter woman. She feels betrayed by our father. I always assumed that he cheated on her with your mother, but he swore to me that he didn't meet Eleanor until a year after he divorced my mom."

"Do you believe him?"

Austin shrugged. "I have no way of knowing one way or the other, but I guess it doesn't matter now."

"I think that it does matter to you."

He met Jordin's gaze. "Why did you say that?"

"Because you need to know if you can trust your father. You need to know if he'd being honest with you. I would want to know the truth."

"What do you think?" Austin inquired.

"I believe my father," she responded, "and my mother. She has always told us that she and Dad met after his divorce."

"I guess he's telling the truth, then."

"Austin, why did you really come to Charleston?" Jordin asked. "I believe that our father is part of the reason, but I have a feeling there's more to this story."

"You're right," he admitted. "There is something I haven't told you or Dad."

"What's going on with you?"

"I have a son," Austin announced. "He's the other reason I came to Charleston. I found out that he's here."

A soft gasp escaped her. "Wow…"

"I only found out about the child a couple of months ago. His mother gave him up for adoption, so I decided to look for him. I don't want him growing up feeling that his biological father abandoned him."

"You knew nothing of the adoption?" Jordin inquired.

"I had no knowledge of the pregnancy. I would have been there for my child."

The tenderness in his expression amazed her. "Is there anything I can do to help?"

Austin shook his head no. "I want to handle this on my own."

She reached over and hugged her brother. "I'm here if you need me. We're family."

"I would appreciate if you just keep this between us for now, Jordin."

She nodded in understanding. "I won't say anything."

"Thank you." He paused a heartbeat before saying, "I hear you're seeing someone."

Jordin broke into a wide grin. "It's not like that. A childhood friend recently moved back here and I reconnected with him."

"From the expression on your face, I can see that you care a great deal for this man."

She smiled. "Is it that obvious?"

Austin gave a slight nod.

"To be honest, I feel that he's my soul mate… I know it sounds corny."

He smiled. "Not when you're a romantic."

"Are you telling me that you believe in love everlasting?" Jordin inquired with a grin.

"I believe it's possible."

"So do I."

"Does the guy feel the same way about you?" Austin asked.

"He's been through a lot which has left him pretty guarded. I know that he cares about me, but he hasn't acted on those feelings yet."

"Give him time."

Jordin agreed. "He has some emotional scars that need to heal, so I plan to give him all the space he needs for now."

"If he has any sense, he won't let you go without a fight."

"Thanks, big brother."

Austin headed toward the door, then stopped. He turned around and said, "You and Jadin have been wonderful to me. I'm lucky to have you two as sisters."

"I hope that you know we feel the same way about you, Austin. We love you."

"You hardly know me."

"It doesn't matter. We're family," Jordin responded. "We have always loved you because you are a part of us."

"I can't say the same," he confessed. "I once resented you both."

She shrugged in nonchalance. "I understand why you felt that way, but it doesn't matter. It doesn't change my love for you."

"Like I said, I'm lucky to have such wonderful sisters."

"How are things with you and your mom?"

"She's still a little upset about my being here, but there's nothing she can do about it."

"Does she know about your child?"

"Not yet," Austin responded. "I don't want to get her hopes up about a grandchild she may never get the chance to meet."

"Let me know if I can do anything to help you with this, Austin. I mean it."

"I'll let you know."

Jordin checked her watch. "Hey, how about having lunch with me?"

"Sure."

They left the office and walked to the café on the corner.

She felt a tap on her shoulder while waiting to be seated and turned around. "Ethan, how are you?"

"I'm fine." His gaze traveled over to her brother. She thought she detected something in his gaze, but it disappeared as quickly as it had come. "This is my brother, Austin."

"It's nice to meet you," Ethan said as he shook Austin's hand.

"Same here."

"Would you like to join us for lunch?" Jordin inquired.

"I would love to, but I'm actually on my way to the gym," Ethan responded with a smile. "I have a staff meeting."

When they were seated, Austin stated, "So Ethan is the man you consider your soul mate."

Jordin met her brother's gaze. "How did you know that?"

"Because you were giving Ethan that look that says you adore everything about him."

She laughed. "I was not."

"In case you didn't know—you wear your feelings for the world to see."

Jordin met her brother's gaze. "I can say the same thing about you, Austin."

"It must be a DuGrandpre trait."

They both laughed.

She picked up her menu, although she knew what she wanted to eat.

"Mind if we join you?" Jadin asked.

"Sure," Jordin said, surprised by the appearance of her sister and Ryker.

She and Austin made room for them.

"Kem is coming to town in a couple of weeks," Ryker announced. "Why don't we all get tickets to see him? He is still my favorite singer. We haven't had a next generation outing in a while."

Austin glanced over at her. "Next generation?"

"We're the next generation," she explained. "We all get together and just hang out. Sometimes we go bowling... attend concerts...whatever."

"Sounds like fun." Austin laid down his menu. "I'm in."

"So am I," Jordin interjected.

"Me too," Jadin said. "Have you spoken to Aubrie?"

Ryker nodded. "She's in."

Jordin decided this was something she needed to take her mind off Ethan. Plus, a night out with her family—she was looking forward to a great time. She felt a certain sadness that Ethan and his mother were estranged. She prayed time would heal the rift between him and Lydia.

Jordin's perfume attacked Ethan's nostrils, casting a spell of seduction, causing his heartbeat to throb in his ears. He couldn't seem to tear his gaze away as Jordin made confident strides across the hardwood floor, her hips swaying gently as she walked.

The warning look her brother gave him was not missed by Ethan. He knew that Austin hadn't always been in Jordin's life, but he was obviously very protective of his sibling. Ethan found that his feelings for Jordin wouldn't just go away. Every time he saw her, he wanted to reach out and pull her into his arms. He could never forget the intensity of her incredible, warm brown eyes and smooth complexion.

What is wrong with me?

Ethan's pulse skittered alarmingly. He was knocked off guard by his response to Jordin. Never had he experienced anything so powerful. None of this made much sense to him. He went to the gym for a quick work out before his meeting with Walter.

Two hours later, Ethan returned to his office.

"This just came for you," his assistant announced as he entered through the double doors.

He tore his thoughts off Jordin and skimmed the papers that were just handed to him. The white, sealed envelope caught his attention.

Bile rose up in Ethan's throat. The letter was from his mother.

He stood stiffly in front of the huge window, his head reeling from the unexpected letter he was holding.

After a moment, Ethan tossed the letter into his wastebasket.

He sat down at his desk and began returning phone calls. It was better that he kept busy. It helped to focus on the business at hand.

His mother and her letter forgotten, Ethan spent the rest of the afternoon taking care of items on his checklist. If things continued along this vein, he would leave by five o'clock. He hadn't been able to do that in a while.

Ethan didn't leave his office until five thirty. He went by the house to see how much progress had been made in the renovations before heading to the hotel.

For the first time in a very long time, Ethan experienced the ache of loneliness.

Chapter 8

The next day, Jordin tucked her hair behind her ears as she spied Ethan walking toward her on Broad Street. She was once again taken with how utterly and completely handsome he was. Just as he seemed to take over any room he entered—Ethan seemed to take over the street as he strode along the sidewalk.

"It's a crime for a man to look so good," she murmured under her breath.

He broke into a huge smile as he shortened the distance between them. "Hey, beautiful."

She greeted him with a hug. "Where are you headed?"

"I heard there was a nice little deli two blocks away," Ethan responded. "I figured I'd give it a try."

"Get the grilled chicken sandwich," she suggested. "It's delicious."

"Where are you going?"

"To the courthouse."

"Do you have time for lunch?" Ethan inquired.

She hated to turn him down, but she had eaten earlier. "I actually just had a salad, but thanks for the invitation."

"I have another invite for you," he announced. "My grand opening is coming up next week. I hope you plan on attending."

Jordin smiled. "Definitely. Jadin and I have already made plans to be there."

Ethan escorted her to the parking lot. "I'll give you a call later to see if you're up for some company."

"Come on over," Jordin stated. "I'm not doing anything special."

"I'll bring pizza."

"Sounds great."

The day could not come to an end soon enough for her. She and Ethan always had a good time together. They talked a lot about the past, but Jordin longed to know more about his years away. She didn't want to push him too hard. She needed to make him comfortable enough to let down his guard around her completely.

The more time she spent with him, the more he seemed at ease.

In her heart, Jordin knew everything would work out perfectly. Ethan would wake up and realize that they belonged together.

She left work shortly after five.

Jordin had enough time to get home, shower and change into a pair of leggings beneath an oversize sweatshirt before Ethan arrived.

"Hey…" she greeted him with a smile, opening the door wide enough to let him enter.

"You still love pepperoni and bacon on your pizza?"

Jordin nodded. "I sure do."

She already had plates on the table. "Let's eat."

"We need some music," Ethan said.

"My iPod's over there on the counter," Jordin told him.

"You have Pandora?"

She laughed. "Yes. Who doesn't?"

He shrugged. "I don't know. You tend to follow your own beat."

"I'm not the only one," she retorted as she placed two slices of pizza on her plate.

Ethan did the same.

Jordin blessed the food.

She bit into a slice. "I have missed this so much."

He frowned. "You stopped eating pizza?"

"I've been eating veggie pizza—it's what Jadin likes. When we have our girls' night, we order that one. That's about the only time I eat pizza these days."

"I love this song..." Jordin began swaying to the music and singing. She gestured for Ethan to join her.

He wiped his mouth and chimed in for the chorus.

She rose to her feet and began dancing.

He followed suit.

"Ain't no mountain high enough..." they sang in unison.

When the song ended, they returned to their chairs, collapsing in laughter.

"That used to be our song, remember?" Jordin asked.

"Every time I hear it, I think of you," he confessed.

"What was the other song we used to sing...the one by The Jackson 5?"

"'I'll Be There.'"

Jordin grinned. "I love hearing you sing that song. You thought you were Michael Jackson."

"No, I thought I sang it better than Michael," Ethan said with a chuckle.

"You could've given him a run for his money."

He threw back his head laughing. "That's what I love about you, Jordin. You have always had my back. If I told you I could fly to the moon without a rocket—you'd encourage me to do it."

"I'm your personal cheerleader," she responded. "Ethan, I know you'd do the same for me. You even got a black eye for me. I told you I could handle that boy, but you had to be my hero."

"How would it look if I'd let you try and fight that knucklehead? I got tired of him trying to push up on you. That day, he was trying to take you into the gym—I lost it."

"My hero…" she murmured.

"Come to think of it, you saved me that time when that girl wanted to fight me because I didn't want to go to the Sadie Hawkins dance with her."

"That's right… I forgot her name but she was mad with you."

"I wasn't even rude when I turned her down. I just didn't want to go."

"I know," Jordin stated. "You turned me down too. If you'd said yes to me, then I wouldn't have had to threaten to knock her out when she started throwing rocks at you."

Ethan laughed. "She had good aim too."

Jordin nodded in agreement. "She tagged me one of those times."

"So that's the real reason you went after her," he teased. "Because she hit you with a rock. I thought you were protecting me."

Laughing, she shook her head no. "I was going to beat her down for the both of us."

Ethan threw back his head and laughed. "That chick was crazy."

"Yeah, I heard that the next day at school," Jordin responded. "Everyone was saying how shocked they were to see me after tangling with her. I just knew she would be gunning for me but she didn't—she stayed as far away from me as possible." She chuckled. "Talk about thankful."

Their eyes met and held.

"Those were the good old days, huh?"

"The good ol' days," she murmured softly.

Jordin spent most of the morning convincing her sister to attend the grand opening of Ethan's Boot Camp Gym. "I told him that you and I planned to come together."

"Why did you do that?"

"Jadin, you owe me for the night I went with you to that sushi restaurant." They both discovered that they were not fans of this particular type of food. She didn't regret the experience however. She enjoyed her time with her sister and they had tried something new together.

"Okay, I'll go."

Jordin sighed with relief. "You're going to have a good time. I know how much you miss Michael and sitting at home alone is not going to make you feel any better."

"You're right, sis."

"I'll pick you up at three."

"See you then," Jadin replied.

Jordin padded barefoot to her walk-in closet after hanging up the telephone. She picked out a couple of outfits before deciding on one.

Three hours later, they were on their way to the gym.

"Thanks for coming with me, Jadin."

"Not a problem," she responded. "I'm really having a great time. I've already signed up for a class."

When Ethan joined them, Jordin said, "This is a really nice gym."

Jadin nodded in agreement. "It's good to see you, Ethan."

"Thank you for coming," he said as he embraced Jadin.

"Congratulations, Ethan. I would sign up for membership if I were more exercise-minded."

Jordin glanced at her sister. "I can't remember the last time I saw you in a gym."

"It's been a couple of years," Jadin confessed.

"My gyms are for those who want to take their workouts to the next level."

"That's definitely not me," Jadin responded. "If you two don't mind, I'm going to make my way over to the buffet table."

When they were alone, Jordin glanced down at the schedule in her hand. "These programs seem pretty rigorous."

"Still think that you're up for boot camp?" Ethan asked, a grin on his face.

"Of course," Jordin responded. "In fact, I want to try the cardio kickboxing class." She was never one to back down from a challenge. "What is Tabata training?"

"It's a high-intensity training technique," Ethan explained. "We use twenty-second bursts of maximum-intensity work with a ten-second rest period. We repeat it eight times in a row. Tabata training can be done with barbells, kettlebells or just body-weight exercises."

"I don't think I'm ready for this class."

He laughed. "That might be a good idea. Do you work out regularly?"

"I do," she answered. "Three days a week."

"What's your routine?"

"I take kickboxing on Monday, cycling on Wednesday and aerobics on Friday."

"Okay, sounds like you're ready to go to the next level. If you're serious about this, give Walter a call and he'll schedule a session for you with one of our trainers."

"I really want to give this a try."

"I thought you and Jadin would be less identical as you got older, but looking at the two of you now—it's the opposite."

Jordin met his gaze. "Her hair is lighter than mine but other than that, we are mirror images."

"I'm glad that you came."

"I wouldn't be anywhere else, Ethan."

She looked up at him and found his attention was somewhere else.

"I can't believe this..." he mumbled.

"What is it?" Jordin glanced over her shoulder.

"Lydia..."

Jordin turned around to find Ethan's mother standing a few yards away.

"Excuse me. I need to take care of this," he uttered.

Before she could respond, Ethan was gone. Jordin watched as he walked briskly across the floor toward his mother.

"Is that Mrs. Holbrooke?" Jadin asked, coming to stand beside her. "She's so thin."

"That's her."

"Ethan doesn't seem happy at all about her being here."

"Things between them are very strained and she really wants to work out her relationship with Ethan."

"Unfortunately, he doesn't appear to be interested," Jadin stated. "He looks very angry with her."

"That's what makes this so sad," Jordin responded. "She's his mother and they need to talk so they can sort things out."

Her eyes traveled the room, searching for Ethan, but he had disappeared off somewhere.

"Why don't you go talk to him?" Jadin suggested.

"I think I will," Jordin responded. "Grab some more to eat and I'll be back shortly."

She walked toward the office located at the back of the gym.

"I was just looking for you," Jordin stated when she saw him inside.

"I needed to be alone for a moment," he responded.

"Your mother is still here."

Ethan released a soft sigh. "I guess there is no avoiding this."

"Are you going to talk to her?" Jordin inquired.

He gave a slight nod. "I need to get this over with."

"Why don't you bring her back here?" Jordin suggested. "I'm sure you don't want to have a discussion in front of your guests."

Ethan agreed. "I'll have Walter bring her back in a few minutes."

"I'll be with Jadin. Let me know if you want to talk after the opening."

Ethan nodded.

Jordin hugged him. "It's going to be fine."

Deep down, she wasn't so sure. Ethan was not happy at all over this turn of events. She prayed Lydia's appearance had not ruined his celebration.

"What are you doing here?" Ethan demanded, attempting to keep his voice low when his mother entered the office.

His mother boldly met his gaze. "You refuse to take my calls, son." She pulled on the dress she wore, which looked too big for her slight frame. She clutched a purse that had seen better days close to her chest.

"Then you should've taken the hint. Lydia, I've tried to make it clear that I don't want to talk to you."

She glanced over her shoulder, then back at him. "How can you treat me this way?"

"I'm not doing this right now," he said in a loud whisper. "Please leave now or I will have security escort you out, Lydia. We have nothing to discuss."

"Ethan, I'm your mother."

"Let me make myself clear. I no longer need a mother. You had your chance and you chose Rob over your own son. Well, it's too late to change that now."

"Just give me a chance to explain."

"I need to attend to my guests. I'm going to call you a taxi." He took out his wallet and handed her fifty dollars. "This should more than cover the fare."

"I didn't come here for your money."

"Do you have any cash?" he asked.

Lydia shook her head no.

"Take the money," he insisted.

"I'll leave for now, son, but I want you to know that I'm not giving up."

"Do yourself a favor and go on with your life…without me. Walter will come get you when the taxi gets here."

"I can't," she told him, a lone tear sliding down her cheek. "I will do whatever I have to do, Ethan. You may not need me but I need you in my life."

"Why don't you just call up Rob? Or is he still in prison?"

Before she could respond, Ethan walked out of the office.

He wanted nothing to do with her.

"Is everything okay?" Jordin asked when he walked up to her.

"It is now," he responded. "I've called a taxi for Lydia."

"Things looked very intense between you and your mother."

"Hopefully, that's the last time I'll see her."

Stunned by his words, Jordin gasped. "Ethan, you don't mean that."

He met her gaze. "Yes, I do."

"She is your *mother.*"

He shrugged "I don't need her in my life."

Jordin could hear the pain in his voice, although Ethan was trying to sound nonchalant. Somewhere deep down, he still loved his mother very much. He was just too angry to realize it right now.

Her eyes traveled the room, searching for her sister. Jadin was near the buffet table talking to some guy who looked like a body builder. He was probably one of the trainers who worked here at the gym.

"You have any plans later?" he asked.

Jordin shook her head. "No, not a thing. What's up?"

"I was thinking we could catch a movie or something."

She looked up at him and smiled. "Sure."

"We can see something near your house," Ethan told her.

"That's fine."

Jordin and Jadin left half an hour later. During the drive home, Jordin said, "Looks like you made a new friend."

"I guess you saw me talking to Jack. He seems like a nice guy."

She gave her a sidelong glance. "Did he ask you out?"

Jadin smiled. "He did, but I turned him down. I told him that I was seeing someone."

"I thought you and Michael were calling it quits."

"We have," her sister confirmed. "I'm not ready to start dating someone new, however."

"Ethan and I are going to the movies later," Jordin announced.

"I guess things are going well between you two."

"Disappointed?" she asked with a chuckle.

Jadin laughed. "I'm not doing this with you. I know how much it thrills you to prove me wrong."

After she dropped her sister off at home, Jordin made her way to her own house.

Ethan arrived just before seven o'clock.

She took one look at him and asked, "Do you want to talk about it?"

"About what?" he asked.

"What happened with your mother earlier," Jordin responded. "We don't have to go out anywhere if you're not feeling up to it. We can order some food and just hang out here."

"There's not much to discuss," Ethan said as he settled down on the sofa. "Lydia wants to pick up from where we left off and it's not going to happen."

"This shouldn't come as a surprise to you since she's your mom. Why are you being so stubborn about this, Ethan?"

"Because Lydia chose a man over her own child. She knew transporting drugs was against the law. All that stuff she used to spout about the dangers of using drugs… what a hypocrite."

"She's served her time in prison for her crime. Don't you think people deserve second chances?"

"Jordin, I know what you're trying to do, but it's not going to work. Nothing will ever change the truth."

"You don't think you can ever forgive her?"

Ethan shook his head. "I can't. Jordin, I don't expect you to understand what I'm dealing with—your parents have always been there for you. My mother had an affair with a man who was engaged to someone else. She got pregnant with me to try and trap my dad, but it backfired. He went through with his wedding." Ethan shook his head sadly. "Parents don't think of how their actions affect their children."

"Look at all you've accomplished in spite of everything," Jordin pointed out.

"That's because I refused to let my past define the man I became."

"Do you have a relationship with your father now?"

"No," Ethan responded. "We talk every now and then, but it's not what I would consider a relationship. He only started calling after I became wealthy. All of a sudden, I was good enough to be a part of the family. His wife never wanted me around, but she wants me to pay college tuition for her daughters."

"Did you do it?"

He nodded. "I pay it directly to the school. They have nothing to do with the drama that existed between our parents."

"I hope they appreciate what you're doing?"

"It doesn't matter if they do or not," Ethan uttered. "I'm doing what I believe is right."

"What does your brother do?" Jordin wanted to know.

"Trey is in the military. I can't believe you remember him?" It had been almost twenty years since his father brought his half brother to Charleston so they could meet.

Jordin ordered Chinese food while Ethan searched for something to watch on television. They decided to just spend the evening at her place.

He removed his shoes.

"I'm glad to see you're getting comfortable."

Ethan laughed.

"The food should be here soon," Jordin announced as she settled down beside him. "I heard everything you said earlier, Ethan."

He looked at her. "I feel like there's a *but* coming."

"I remember how close you two used to be."

"That was a long time ago, Jordin," he responded quietly.

"You may be angry with your mom, but you still love her."

Ethan shifted his position, but did not comment.

"In time, you two will talk and all of this will be just a memory."

"Some things do not come with a happy ending, Jordin." His tone was velvet, yet edged with steel.

She glimpsed the pain in his eyes.

Jordin reached over and covered his hand with her own. "Have faith."

"Forever the optimist."

"Try it sometime."

A smile tugged at his lips. "You used to tell me that when we were sixteen."

"Obviously, you still need a reminder," Jordin said with a grin.

Their gazes met and held.

She tried to assess his unreadable features.

"Did you find anything on television?" she asked, putting an end to the silence.

Ethan handed her the remote. "I'll let you choose. We can skip through the arguing."

She tossed a pillow at him. "You love romantic comedies too."

"Actually, I don't," he responded. "I just give in."

"Okay, so let's do something different. We will watch anything you pick out."

"Really?"

Jordin nodded. She was already regretting her decision, but kept quiet.

Ethan turned to the channel guide and scrolled down. "Let's watch this."

"*Mystical Journey: Kumbh Mela,*" she uttered. "Really?"

He gave her a sidelong glance. "Yeah. Sounds interesting, don't you think?"

"You don't even know what this is about."

"It's the largest religious festival in the world," Ethan replied.

She chuckled. "I read that as well."

"Hindus on a pilgrimage of faith gather to bathe in a sacred river. Last year it was held in Haridwar."

"Okay, let's watch it, then."

Ethan glanced over at her. "You're sure?"

"Yes," Jordin responded. She was not about to back down.

Thirty minutes into the documentary, she fell asleep, her head on Ethan's chest. He had fallen asleep fifteen minutes earlier.

Jordin smiled sleepily. She had outlasted him.

Chapter 9

Ethan woke up and tried to move. Jordin was snuggled against him sleeping soundly. He checked his watch.

It was almost five in the morning.

He stretched his legs while trying to figure out a way to move Jordin without waking her. Gathering her in his arm, he held her snugly.

Ethan turned off the television.

He relished the feel of her body next to his, her nearness making his senses spin while giving him a measure of comfort. Ethan felt the movement of Jordin's breathing.

At some point, he must have fallen asleep because when Ethan checked his watch again, it was seven o'clock.

Jordin shifted, waking up in the process. "Hey..." she murmured. "What time is it?"

"Seven."

She sat up straight. "In the morning?"

"Yeah."

"Oh, wow," she uttered. "This is the first time we've ever spent the night together."

He gave a short laugh. "Do I get breakfast?"

Fingering through her curls, Jordin responded, "Sure."

She rose to her feet. "Just so you know, I found the documentary enlightening. It just wasn't what I was looking to watch last night."

"I thought it was pretty interesting."

"Ethan, you were the first one to fall asleep."

He laughed. "You're right. Maybe if I'd watched it when I wasn't so tired."

"You can freshen up in the guest bathroom," Jordin stated. "I'm going to take a quick shower."

An hour later, they were seated at the breakfast table.

"What's on your agenda for today?" Ethan inquired.

"We're having a family dinner. It's to celebrate Austin." Jordin stuck a forkful of scrambled eggs in her mouth.

"Your brother seems pretty cool."

She wiped her mouth on a napkin. "He is," Jordin confirmed. "He and my dad are working to build a relationship after all these years."

"I hope it works out for them." A flash of sadness washed over him, but Ethan refused to let it flood his mind.

"What are your plans for today?" she asked.

"I'm going to be at the gym," Ethan stated. "I want to make sure that Walter and his team have everything running smoothly." Checking his watch, he added, "I need to get going. I want to shower and change."

Jordin walked him to the front door. "Call me later, if you're not too busy."

"Enjoy being with your family," he said. Once more,

Ethan felt an ache at the mention of family. *I don't need anyone*, he repeated over and over silently. *I have a good life.*

The thought seemed as hollow as he felt.

After dinner, Jordin sat on the patio along with Jadin and Austin while the other members of her family were inside the house.

"Your mom is a great cook."

"She loves cooking," Jadin said. "Mom and Aubrie are always experimenting with different ingredients."

"Tell me something," Austin interjected. "What's up with your aunt?"

Jordin and Jadin burst into laughter.

He looked from one to the other. "What's so funny?"

"You do know that she is also your aunt," Jordin stated. "Aunt Rochelle is very opinionated and she doesn't mind sharing her thoughts."

"I figured that out pretty quickly. She made it very clear that she never liked my mother."

"There are few people that Aunt Rochelle seems to really like. She's good at what she does, but she can be abrasive. She only has a couple of friends."

"How does your mom deal with her?" Austin wanted to know.

"She ignores her mostly," Jordin responded with a chuckle. "My mom's quiet, but she doesn't take anything off my aunt."

"I like Eleanor," Austin said after a moment. "She's been very welcoming toward me."

"You're family," Jadin stated.

"I have another question," Austin told them. "How many times did you all get lost in this house?"

They laughed.

"It's really not a complicated house," Jordin responded. "There are only bedrooms and bathrooms upstairs. Dad and Mom have separate offices. There's a media room, and bowling alley."

"They love bowling," Jadin contributed.

Jordin shifted her position on the lounge chair. "Austin, have you met anyone yet?"

He smiled. "I've met a couple of girls."

"So you're dating?" Jadin questioned.

Austin shook his head no. "Not really. One is just a friend and the other one—we went on one date, and then she was ready to dive into a serious relationship."

Jordin's eyes widened in surprise. "Whoa…"

"That's what I said."

"You definitely need to stay away from her," Jadin stated. "She sounds like a fatal attraction."

"I hope she's not crazy, but she is pushing hard for a relationship. I was informed that she wants to get married within the next couple of years."

"Austin, you should probably leave her alone," Jordin warned.

"I did," he responded with a chuckle. "We only had the one date, but she calls and texts me almost every day. I've never met a woman so pushy."

The conversation they were having prompted Jordin to consider her relationship with Ethan. He stirred certain emotions within her, but she was careful to avoid getting ahead of herself. Jordin didn't want to set herself up for heartbreak.

"In order to get the best results you have to be able to keep up your momentum for Tabata training," Ethan was saying. "Most people can't."

Jordin folded her arms across her chest. "I thought you

said it was only a four-minute workout. I'm sure I can manage that short amount of time, Ethan."

"Tabata training is the single most effective high-intensity interval training—it is also the most rigorous. Four minutes may seem short, but I'm warning you—it's going to feel much longer than that."

"I'm up to the challenge."

Ethan smiled. "If you really want to try it, then I suggest going light with the weights until you find your range. I'll help you because I don't want you begging people to help you off the floor."

She scrunched up her face. "As if…"

"I forgot how stubborn you can be once you make up your mind to do something."

Jordin broke into a grin.

"This is not something you do daily, Jordin. Most people add this to their workout routine once or twice a week."

"Okay." She looked up at him, meeting his gaze. "I'm ready."

When she pulled out a pair of pink-and-black workout gloves, Ethan chuckled. "I guess you came prepared."

"Ethan, if you're not going to take me seriously, then I want to work with someone else. I didn't come here just to hang around you."

"Okay, sorry."

She studied his face for a moment. "Let's get started."

"I'm going to start you with the most basic method which is twenty seconds of hard training followed by ten seconds of rest. You will repeat this eight times."

When Jordin nodded, he continued. "I'm going to start you with kettlebell swings."

Ethan stood in a wide stance. "I want you to do what I'm doing."

She followed his instructions.

"Be sure to make space for the kettlebell to swing backward. The wide stance gives you stability during the upper portion of the lift."

Four minutes later, Jordin just wanted to fall on the floor in a puddle.

Handing her a bottle of water, Ethan inquired, "Are you okay?"

"I m-made it," she managed.

He smiled. "I'm proud of you, Jordin. I admit that I had my doubts, but you came through like a champ."

She fumbled with the bottle, trying to unscrew the top.

Ethan saw her dilemma and took it from her. "Let me help you."

"Thank you."

Jordin reached for the water and drank. "Wow…" she uttered after a moment. "I thought I was going to die."

"I told you it was intense."

She looked up at him. "That had to be longer than four minutes, Ethan."

He shook his head. "It wasn't."

Jordin struggled to recover. "It was a great workout."

"You're sure you feel okay?" Ethan inquired.

"I'm fine."

He walked her to the women's locker room. "Come by the office before you leave."

"Okay," she responded with a smile.

Jordin was grateful to have a few minutes alone. She sat down on a nearby bench and groaned softly. *I'm not doing this for Ethan. I'm doing this for me.* She exercised on a regular basis, but wanted to take it up a notch. She had certainly done this—she did a self-check to ensure that this was not about Ethan. She didn't want to be one of those girls who were desperate to do anything to get a man's attention. Sure, she wanted to support Ethan, but this was about her personal health goals.

Okay, I probably wouldn't be here if it wasn't for him, she confessed in her heart. *But I'm not desperate—I'm health-conscious.*

Chapter 10

Her body screaming in protest, Jordin crawled out of bed and padded barefoot to the shower. "This sucks to be so sore," she muttered.

Jordin showered and dressed in a pair of sweats. Her hair was damp from her shower, so she allowed it to hang freely in soft ringlets. She was working from home today and it was a good thing too. Jordin could barely walk.

Her telephone rang.

"How are you feeling?" Ethan asked when she answered.

She groaned.

"Did you soak in your tub like I told you last night?"

"I did," Jordin responded. "Please tell me it gets better."

"If you don't feel the burn, then you're not doing it right."

"I'm working from home today thankfully."

"Make sure to soak in the tub today at some point," Ethan said. "It will ease some of the soreness."

"I will."

"I'm concerned so I wanted to check on you."

"I'll live," Jordin murmured. "Thanks for the call."

"Do you have plans for the weekend?"

"I'm going to a concert on Saturday night with Ryker, Jadin, Aubrie and Austin. It's our next-generation outing."

"You all still do that?" Ethan questioned.

"Yes," she responded. "It's been a while since we've all gotten together, but we try to hang out several times throughout the year."

"Chandler and I are going to drive to Hilton Head. He's playing golf for some charity event."

"You don't play golf?" Jordin inquired, noting the less-than-thrilled tone of his voice.

"You know that I've never liked golf."

She gave a slight shrug. "It's been a while. You could have changed your mind."

"Not about that," he uttered.

"When will you be back?"

"Late Sunday evening," Ethan responded. "Have fun with your family."

Jordin smiled. "You have fun on the golf course."

"I doubt it."

She laughed.

They talked a few minutes more before hanging up.

She rubbed the painful muscles in her arms as she went downstairs to get her laptop out of her tote.

Jordin smiled as she pictured Ethan standing around on a golf course. He was going to be miserable.

Jordin and Ethan walked out of the movie theater, heading toward his car. He had called her earlier in the day and invited her out. They had not been able to really connect because he was busy and she'd had a heavy caseload this week.

"I'm so glad you invited me to come to the movies," she murmured. "This has been a long week."

He agreed. "How was the concert?"

"We had a great time. I love Kem's music." Jordin glanced up at him. "How was your weekend in Hilton Head?"

"Those two days felt longer than this entire week," Ethan responded.

She bit back her laughter. "I'm sorry."

"Hilton Head was nice though," he said, opening the door for her.

Ethan drove to her place.

"Coming in?" Jordin inquired.

"Sure."

He sat down in the family room while she retrieved something light for them to eat.

She joined him a few minutes later with a plate of cheese and crackers, which she set down on the coffee table. "I'll be right back with some plates and the wine."

When she returned, Jordin sat down beside Ethan. "How did you like the movie?"

He sat up and reached for his wineglass. "I thought it was great."

"So did I," Jordin replied. "I was kind of surprised that you would pick this one, especially with all of the romantic elements."

Ethan met her gaze. "I knew you would like it."

She smiled. "You were right. It was the perfect movie."

He took a long sip of wine. "I had my doubts about moving back here, but I have to say now that I'm glad I did."

"So I assume you'll be staying around for a while then."

"Yeah. I'd forgotten how much I love Charleston."

Jordin grinned. "I'm glad you're going to be here." She picked up a plate and filled it with cheese and crackers.

"The only issue with being back here is Lydia," Ethan remarked.

"Maybe not right now, Ethan, but one day you might change your mind."

He shook his head. "I doubt that."

A hushed quiet settled over the room.

Without warning, Ethan pulled her closer to him.

He took her mouth as if it was his to do with as he pleased, making it his own in a way that had Jordin's hands rising of their own volition, her fingers curling into his shirt. Her moan slid free of her mouth and into Ethan's.

The kiss was explosive, consuming and intense.

All Jordin could think about was the heat of Ethan's body against her own.

Ethan released her slowly, leaving Jordin breathless, hungry for more of his kisses and drowning in desire.

He drew a slow breath.

She gazed into his chocolate-brown eyes.

"You are irresistible," he murmured, as though having reached some internal understanding with himself. Ethan lowered his head down to hers, and pressed a single kiss on her lips.

Their gazes locked. Jordin and Ethan glimpsed the attraction mirrored in the other's eyes.

Ethan kissed her again, lingering, savoring every moment.

Jordin's emotions whirled. Blood pounded in her brain, leapt from her heart and made her knees tremble.

"I have always been drawn to you, sweetheart," Ethan whispered. "From the moment I laid eyes on you." He touched his lips to hers.

Jordin surrendered to him, her entire body trembling as his arms drew her closer to him. She could feel the heat of passion radiating from within. She wanted him.

Needed him.

Just when Jordin was ready to fully succumb to his seduction, Ethan broke the kiss and picked her up, causing her to gasp softly. He carried her into the bedroom and set her on the bed.

They stared at one another.

"Jordin." He whispered her name, needing to hear permission.

She didn't tear her gaze away as she whispered, "I want this too."

A shudder moved through him.

He pulled away from her abruptly, which prompted her to inquire, "What's wrong, Ethan?"

"On second thought, I don't think it's a good idea for us to get carried away," he said after a moment.

Jordin felt as if part of her soul vanished when Ethan tore himself away from her.

"Ethan…"

He shook his head. "We can't do this, Jordin. It would be a mistake."

"It's what we both want."

He shook his head sadly. "I'm messed up, Jordin and the last thing I want is to hurt you."

"You won't," she responded. "I know *you*, Ethan. I know your heart."

"I've changed a lot, Jordin."

"Not really. You are still the same person I knew all those years ago—only better."

Ethan laughed, breaking up the awkwardness between them. "Only you would say something like that."

"It's the truth." She pulled away from him when she sat up. "C'mon, Ethan…admit it. You feel the same way about me. We're attracted to each other,"

"We're quite a pair, huh?" Ethan rose to his feet.

"We are," Jordin agreed. "Otherwise, I would probably be offended that you don't want to make love to me."

"Let's be clear," Ethan stated. "It's not that I don't want to make love—I don't want to mess up our friendship."

"I'm thirsty," she announced. "Want something to drink?"

"Just some water. Thanks."

Jordin disappeared off to the kitchen. She returned a few minutes later with two bottles of water and handed one to Ethan, who smiled in gratitude.

As usual, his smile stirred something within her. Jordin unscrewed the top of her water took a quick sip.

"I've always been attracted to you," Ethan confessed.

"Why didn't you ever say anything?" she wanted to know.

"I didn't want to get rejected."

Jordin met his gaze. "I wouldn't have rejected you, Ethan."

"I didn't know that back then. The way things turned out for me, it was probably better this way. Relationships are something I haven't been very good at—I certainly don't want to ruin what we already have."

She eyed him. "Why not take a chance?"

Ethan shook his head no. "It's just not a risk I'm willing to take where you're concerned. You have no idea how special you are to me."

Jordin kissed him. "Sure, I can't change your mind?"

He had to tear himself away from the seductive look

FREE Merchandise is 'in the Cards' for you!

Dear Reader,

We're giving away FREE MERCHANDISE!

Seriously, we'd like to reward you for reading this novel by giving you **FREE MERCHANDISE** worth over $20 retail. And no purchase is necessary!

You see the Jack of Hearts sticker above? Paste that sticker in the box on the Free Merchandise Voucher inside. Return the Voucher today... and we'll send you Free Merchandise!

Thanks again for reading one of our novels—and enjoy your Free Merchandise with our compliments!

Pam Powers

Pam Powers

P.S. Look inside to see what Free Merchandise is **"in the cards"** for you!

YOUR FREE MERCHANDISE INCLUDES...

2 FREE Books **AND** 2 FREE Mystery Gifts

FREE MERCHANDISE VOUCHER

2 FREE
BOOKS
and
2 FREE
GIFTS

Please send my Free Merchandise, consisting of
2 Free Books and **2 Free Mystery Gifts**.
I understand that I am under no obligation to buy
anything, as explained on the back of this card.

168/368 XDL GLYA

Please Print

FIRST NAME

LAST NAME

ADDRESS

APT.#   CITY

STATE/PROV.   ZIP/POSTAL CODE

NO PURCHASE NECESSARY!

K-N16-FMC15

▲ If offer card is missing write to: Reader Service, P.O. Box 1867, Buffalo, NY 14240-1867 or visit www.ReaderService.com ▲

BUSINESS REPLY MAIL
FIRST-CLASS MAIL   PERMIT NO. 717   BUFFALO, NY

POSTAGE WILL BE PAID BY ADDRESSEE

READER SERVICE
PO BOX 1867
BUFFALO NY 14240-9952

NO POSTAGE
NECESSARY
IF MAILED
IN THE
UNITED STATES

she gave him. "You're definitely not making this easy on me."

"To be honest, I don't want to make it easy for you, Ethan. I *know* we would be good together, but until you come to your senses, I guess all we can do right now is watch another movie."

Ethan picked up one of the DVDs on her nightstand and said, "Let's watch this one."

The mere touch of Ethan's hand against her own sent a warming shiver through her, which Jordin tried to ignore. She moved her hand away from his.

He glanced over at her. "Jordin...I don't want things to be uncomfortable between us."

"We're fine, Ethan."

"You sure?"

Jordin awarded him a smile. "We're cool. Let's just watch the movie."

She chewed on her bottom lip and pushed away her fantasies of making love with Ethan. He was determined to keep their relationship platonic, much to her disappointment.

Maybe Jadin was right. Maybe she was wasting her time where Ethan was concerned. He seemed to be able to turn his feelings on and off, but it was not something she was gifted with. Maybe it was time that she faced reality and let go of any dreams of being with Ethan.

Ethan was extremely conscious of where Jordin's flesh touched him. He could barely keep his attention on the movie. He and Jordin talked very little during it, but he felt there was still so much that had been left unsaid.

"So what did you think of it?" Jordin asked after the movie ended. "All of the blood and gore."

"It was... I enjoyed it."

Jordin shook her head no. "Terrence Howard was perfect in the role of policeman. I really like him."

"I'm sure most women feel the same way as you do about him. Don't get me wrong—he's a good actor."

"Hater..."

Ethan laughed.

"I have to say this," Jordin blurted. "Ethan, I heard you, but I can't switch my feelings on and off. And I can't just dismiss what almost happened between us earlier. It's going to take me some time. I just need you to know that."

"Jordin...this isn't easy for me either. The things that you do to me...the way you make me feel," Ethan shook his head. He feared if he stayed a moment longer, his resolve would evaporate.

As if she knew what he was thinking, Jordin said, "I guess it's time you head home, then."

He nodded in agreement. "This is for the best, Jordin."

"I don't agree," she retorted.

"I'll call you sometime tomorrow."

"That's fine," she murmured while escorting him to the front door. "Drive safe."

He embraced her.

This time Jordin pulled away first. "I'll talk to you tomorrow."

Alone, she ascended the stairs to her bedroom.

Jordin opened the door and stared at her bed. She never realized just how cold and lonely it looked until now.

Her lips were still tender from Ethan's passion-filled kisses. Her body temperature hadn't cooled yet, so Jordin decided to take a bubble bath, hoping to ease some of the pent-up tension she felt.

No man had ever made her feel the way Ethan made her feel, his touch leaving her burning with desire.

* * *

At home, Ethan took a cold shower. He was dealing with a battle of his own. He was in love with Jordin and the truth of the matter was that he did not want to lose her. Ethan had no idea when it happened, but it did not really matter. She was the only woman he wanted to spend the rest of his life with.

This is so crazy. I'm in love with my best friend, but I can't tell her. The way Jordin responded to his kisses proved that she was attracted to him as well. Ethan just didn't think it was a good idea to put their friendship at risk.

After slipping on a pair of pajama bottoms and a T-shirt, he settled down on the sofa and turned on the television. When he couldn't find anything that captured his attention, Ethan stood up and walked over to the bed.

Climbing inside, he settled back against the pillows.

Sleep would not come easy. Ethan tossed and turned most of the night. He could not escape the look of disappointment on Jordin's face. She had no idea how much he wanted to be with her, but he'd experienced some negative consequences when it came to friends with benefits. Ethan was not willing to risk his friendship with Jordin for sex.

Chapter 11

Ethan had to go to Chicago for business, leaving Jordin to attend the firm's annual event solo. The rows of seating were garnished with riots of red-and-orange roses arranged with gold ribbons and baby's breath. As usual, her mother did a wonderful job with the decorations and themes each year.

"What's wrong, cousin?" Ryker inquired. "We're at a party. You haven't been yourself all evening." He dropped down into the empty seat beside her.

"I'm fine," Jordin responded before taking a sip of wine.

"Does this have something to do with Ethan? I assumed that he would be here with you."

"He's out of town." She met Ryker's gaze.

"How are things between you two?"

"I know that Ethan cares for me, but he won't allow

himself to act on those feelings. Every time we seem to get close, he finds a way to put distance between us."

"Ethan's been through a lot, Jordin," Ryker reminded her. "The real reason that he came back here is to make peace with his past. He needs time to do just that."

"You've spoken to him?"

Ryker nodded. "I ran into him and Chandler a couple of days ago. We sat down and talked over drinks. He told me what happened with his mom."

"Do you know if he plans on staying in Charleston?" she asked. "Sometimes, I get the feeling that he would rather be anywhere but here."

"I think so, especially since he moved his offices here." Ryker met her gaze.

She nodded. "I really believe that Ethan is my soul mate."

"Then give him the time and space he needs to deal with old wounds," Ryker advised. "If he truly is your soul mate, he will come looking for you."

"He has so much bitterness where his mother is concerned. Sometimes I wonder if he'll be able to bury the past and forgive her. He shuts down when I try to get him to even consider the idea."

"Don't take it personally, cousin. Ethan needs time to confront his demons. Give him that space. He'll come to you when he's ready."

"I wasn't there for him when he really needed me, Ryker," Jordin stated. "I should have sensed that there was something going on with him. I don't want to make that mistake a second time."

"Don't be so hard on yourself. None of us knew all that Ethan was going through back then."

"I just don't understand why he wouldn't tell me," Jordin stated. "We were friends."

"Ethan knows that," Ryker said. "He wanted to be a man. He wanted to take care of himself."

"I suppose you're right."

Ryker rose to his feet. "I need to return to my beautiful wife."

Jordin smiled. "Talk to you later."

"Is this seat taken?"

She turned around. "Ethan, I thought you were in Chicago."

"I was," he responded. "The meeting ended early, so I flew out this afternoon."

"I'm so glad you're here."

He sat down beside her. "Looks like a nice party."

"The law firm throws one every year to celebrate our clients."

Ethan glanced around. "Where are your parents? I'd like to say hello to them."

"They will be back shortly," Jordin stated. "They went to pick up my grandfather."

"Mr. Marcelle DuGrandpre?"

Smiling, she nodded and said, "You remember him."

"Oh, yeah, I remember Mr. Marcelle," Ethan said. "He told me once that if I ever hurt you, he would pistol-whip me."

Jordin laughed. "I wish I could tell you that he didn't mean it, but I'd be lying."

"Oh, I know he meant it."

She glanced over her shoulder. "My parents are here." Jordin stood up and gestured for them to join her.

"Ethan, I heard you were back in town," Eleanor stated. "It's good to see you again and congratulations on the new gym."

"Thank you, Mrs. DuGrandpre."

"I see you and Jordin wasted no time reconnecting."

He smiled. "She's one of my closest friends."

"Ethan's also in need of your services," Jordin said.

"When you have some time, let's get together," Eleanor suggested.

"Ethan Holbrooke, you're the last person I expected to return to Charleston especially after the scandal," a woman's voice interjected.

"Aunt Rochelle..." Jordin uttered in frustration. She loved her aunt dearly, but the woman could be so vexing at times.

She stole a peek at Ethan but his expression was blank. Jordin knew he would never let her aunt know whether or not she hit a nerve.

"Rochelle, why don't you and I check on the cake?" Eleanor suggested. "The delivery truck arrived just as we were pulling in."

"You can check on it. I want to catch up with this young man."

Eleanor gently grabbed her sister-in-law by the arm. "No, I insist that you join me."

"That woman is still a piece of work," Ethan whispered, sparking laughter from Jordin.

She ran her fingers across her gown, a tangerine color.

"You look beautiful," Ethan stated.

"You clean up pretty nice yourself. I don't think I've ever seen you in a tux."

He laughed. "I guess you hadn't."

She was entranced by the silent sadness of his face. Jordin had seen this look a few times and knew he was thinking of the past. She reached over and gave him hand a reassuring squeeze.

"Do you feel like getting some fresh air?" Ethan inquired.

Jordin smiled. "Sure."

A few of the guests were scattered outside the huge estate that belonged to her parents. She and Ethan walked beneath a huge elm tree.

"This place is really pretty at night. I love the way the moon reflects on the waterfront."

He agreed. "This is my first time here."

His words made Jordin realize just how little Ethan had seen of the city of his birth. He had been ripped away before he could get a real glimpse of all that Charleston had to offer.

She glanced up at him to find Ethan watching her.

"Where did you go?"

Jordin met his gaze. "I was thinking about taking you to see all of the wonderful places you never got to see."

"I'd like that. I love spending time with you."

A delicious shudder heated her body. She cleared her throat, pretending not to be affected by his words. "Same here."

For a moment, Jordin thought he was going to kiss her. When he didn't, she felt a shred of disappointment snake down her spine.

"Ready to go back inside?"

She nodded.

Jordin chewed on her bottom lip as Ethan escorted her into the room where the party was held.

He guided her over to their table and pulled out a chair for her.

"Thank you," Jordin murmured as she sat down, her heart hammering foolishly.

I've got to stop this, she told herself. She watched him as he dropped down into the chair beside her, noting how handsome Ethan looked in the black tux he was wearing. It fit him nicely as if it had been designed just for him.

They dined on grilled London broil served with mushroom sauce, vegetables and an assortment of rolls.

Jordin used the corner of her napkin to wipe her mouth. "Do you have any plans for tomorrow?"

"I need to finish unpacking the equipment for my home office. What's up?"

"Nothing," she responded. "I was just being nosy."

He laughed. "What are your plans?"

"Shopping," Jordin answered. "I need some new shoes."

"I doubt that."

"Ethan, I haven't seen you in the same pair of shoes since we reconnected. You love shoes as much as I do."

"I'm sure I don't own near as many as you do."

"Maybe not, but you were a late bloomer. Trust me, you have been bitten by the shoe bug."

They laughed.

"Would you like to dance?" Ethan asked.

She smiled at him. "Sure."

Jordin stood up, waiting for Ethan to escort her to the dance floor. She walked slowly, her body swaying to the music. "I love this song."

Ethan took her to the middle of the front of the dance floor and began moving to the music.

Their eyes locked, sending Jordin's heart hammering against her ribs. He was watching her so intently that she asked, "Why are you staring at me like that?"

"You have no idea how badly I want to kiss you."

She felt her skin become flushed and heated. "It wouldn't bother me if you did."

Just as their lips connected, a photographer snapped a picture of them.

The song ended with him escorting her back to their table.

"You know that picture will probably be on the society page of the newspaper," Ethan blurted. "I'm not sure we should've crossed certain boundaries."

Jordin sighed softly in frustration. Once again, Ethan had erected a wall between them. She only had his best interests at heart and it irritated her that he could not see it this way.

Ethan's heart was racing, his gaze moving over her body slowly. He gave himself a mental shake. Ethan needed to rein in his emotions.

They came from two different worlds.

Ethan had always felt that Etienne DuGrandpre did not think he was good enough for Jordin. Although he had been polite at the party, Ethan was sure Etienne's feelings had not changed.

From outward appearances, Jordin looked fragile, but he knew that she possessed a quiet strength—one of the many qualities that had drawn him to her. Ethan's feelings for her continued to run deep, despite his resolve to keep their relationship a platonic one.

Jordin was the only woman Ethan ever felt connected to—she made him feel things he never felt before. As strong as his feelings were for her, Ethan vowed to stay on the side of caution. The last thing he wanted to do was hurt Jordin. She deserved much better.

Ethan dreaded the idea of seeing her with another man, but it was inevitable. He wanted Jordin to be happy.

"Hey, you..." she prompted. "What's on your mind?"

"I was thinking about us," he confessed.

"Have you changed your mind?"

He shook his head no.

"I see," Jordin responded.

Ethan was mildly surprised that she didn't offer any argument. Perhaps it was because she felt the same way.

"I still don't agree, but we will always be friends, Ethan. No matter what happens."

He smiled. "You told me that same thing years ago."

"I meant it then and I mean it now."

"Feel like some more dancing?" Ethan asked.

Jordin nodded.

Looking at her, Ethan desperately wanted to forget the past and unlock his heart, but it was much too late. He'd realized a long time ago that he would never be completely free of his pain. With his mother in town, Ethan was unable to move forward—she was a constant reminder of all he'd had to endure in her absence.

His gaze traveled to Jordin. She was smiling and dancing, warmth radiating from her.

Ethan allowed himself to be wrapped in that warmness, forcing thoughts of his mother and the past away from his mind.

Jordin's mind was still on Ethan when she arrived home. It was a pleasant surprise when he'd shown up at the party. A quiver surged through her veins as she recalled how much she had enjoyed his company.

"We always have such a nice time together," Jordin whispered to her empty bedroom.

She turned on some music as she undressed.

Humming softly, she slipped on a pair of pajama pants and a matching camisole.

She and Ethan were a good team, she thought as she climbed into bed.

If only he could see it too. Jordin could not understand why it was so difficult for such a brilliant businessman to figure out that a solid friendship was the foundation for love. Why couldn't he see that they were made for each other?

Ethan still dominating her thoughts, Jordin walked over to the window in her bedroom and stared into the night. "I'm so happy that you're back, but Ethan, you're driving me crazy," she whispered. "You know that we were meant to be... I just need you to trust your heart."

Chapter 12

The next day Jordin went to see Ethan at his office. Deep down, she knew that Ryker was right about giving Ethan some space, but she couldn't do it. Jordin wanted to let Ethan know that she would always be there for him.

"Hello, Ethan…"

He smiled. "Somehow, I knew that I'd see you before the week ended. I really enjoyed the party Friday night. It's always good hanging out with you."

"I'm glad to hear that. I want to talk to you about what happened when we were younger. I can't say that I know exactly what you're going through, but you don't have to shut me out. Ethan, I am still your friend and I care about you."

"I know that, Jordin," he responded. "I care about you as well, which is why I don't want to hurt you in any way. I have a lot of baggage which I'm working to get rid of permanently."

"Are you seeing someone to help you with this?"

"As in a psychiatrist?"

She nodded.

He shook his head. "I'm not crazy."

"I know that," Jordin said. "You need to find a way to deal with your *baggage*, as you put it, to keep it from intruding into your present. I have a really good friend who is a psychologist. Her name is Bree Collins. Before you dismiss the idea, at least meet with her and then if you decide it's not for you—it's not an option."

He seemed to be considering her suggestion.

"Just think about it."

"I will."

"I'm going to my parents' house this weekend," Jordin announced. "I'd really like you to come with me."

"I don't know…"

"We're having a nice family dinner. Jadin's bringing her boyfriend and I want you to be my date."

He grinned. "You sure about this?"

Jordin nodded. "Yes. Don't worry, I'll keep Aunt Rochelle as far away from you as possible."

"Is your uncle making his famous seafood gumbo?"

"As a matter of fact, he sure is," she responded. "My mom is making a red velvet cake."

"I haven't tasted a red velvet cake that comes close to your mom's."

"So you'll be my date?"

Ethan nodded. "Sure."

"Just so you know, I heard you the other night. This date is a friend thing."

"I know that you wouldn't try to manipulate me in that way, Jordin."

"We still have a lot of distance between us, so I wanted to make sure you knew my motive."

"I trust you," Ethan told her. "I want you to trust me when I say that I care deeply for you, Jordin. Right now, my being in a relationship with anyone is not a good idea."

"I don't agree with you, but it's not my choice to make," she responded. "I respect your decision. One day, you'll come to your senses, I'm sure."

Ethan burst into laughter. "Same ol' Jordin."

"That's what you love about me," she replied, rising to her feet. "I need to get back to my office."

Ethan stood up and walked from around his desk.

He embraced her. "I'll let you know what I decide."

"I will support you regardless of whatever you decide. I want you to know that."

"I know you will."

Jordin kissed Ethan's cheek. "Give me a call later if you're not busy."

He walked her to the door.

She had actually suggested that he see a therapist. Ethan had considered it once before, but never actually pursued the thought.

Am I really that messed up?

Ethan returned to his office and sat down at his desk. If he wanted to feel normal again, then maybe this was his only option.

Jordin and Ethan drove out to spend the day with Ryker and his family.

Garland greeted them at the front door.

The two women embraced. "Look at you…" Jordin said. "I'm envious of that glow."

"You're just trying to make me feel better about looking like a blimp."

"Jordin's right," Ethan stated. "You look beautiful."

Garland smiled. "I'm so glad you two came over. I'm not getting out much these days. The doctor wants me off my feet as much as possible."

Jordin grabbed her arm, saying, "Well, let's get you over to the couch. We can chat over there."

Ryker entered the room. "Hey...I didn't know y'all were here."

He embraced Jordin first, and then Ethan before taking a seat beside his wife.

"How was the golf tournament?" Ryker inquired.

Ethan shook his head. "I was miserable."

Jordin chuckled. "Let's not even talk about it."

Ryker burst into laughter. "Was it that bad?"

"I hate golf and I hate standing around in the heat watching it even more."

"I'm sure Chandler was in his element though," Ryker stated.

Ethan agreed. "He did well."

"I'm going to get something to drink," Ryker blurted. "You all want anything?"

"I'm fine," his wife responded.

Jordin shook her head. "No thank you."

"I'll take a bottled water."

Ryker strode out of the room, leaving Ethan alone with the women.

"Do you *wressel*?"

Ethan turned and glanced down at the little girl standing beside the chair he was sitting in. He hadn't even heard her approach. "Excuse me?"

"Do you wressel people?"

Jordin and Garland chuckled.

He broke into a grin. "No, I'm not a wrestler."

"You have big muscles."

Ethan replied, "And you have very beautiful eyes."

She giggled. "What's your name?"

"Ethan," he responded. "What's yours?"

"Kai."

"Hey, little lady. Did you forget about me?" Jordin said, holding out her arms for a hug.

"Naw, I didn't forget about you." Kai ran over to her. "I was just talking to *him*."

Jordin sent Ethan a look of amusement. "That's my friend."

Kai looked over at him and said, "He's my friend too. Aren't you?"

"I sure am," he responded, his heart warmed at the sight of her gorgeous brown eyes and head of curly hair. Kai's cheeks were like a cherub's.

She sat down next to Jordin. "I'll be your friend too."

Jordin ran her fingers through Kai's poufy ponytail.

"I think your sister's looking for you, sweetie," Ryker stated when he returned. He handed a bottle of water to Ethan before reclaiming his seat beside Garland. "I heard her calling for you."

"Okay. See you later." She ran off toward the staircase.

"No running," Garland called out. "You have to be careful on the stairs, honey."

"She's adorable," Ethan said to Ryker and Garland. "She was the one at Jordin's parents' house, right?"

Jordin shook her head. "That was Amya."

"Are they twins? They seem to be about the same age."

Garland chuckled. "They are the same age and born on the same day, but they aren't twins."

Ethan's eyebrows rose in surprise. "Interesting…"

"The babies were switched at birth," Ryker elaborated. "Kai is Garland's biological daughter and Amya is mine. We didn't want to give up the children we raised nor our biological children. We decided to coparent them and we fell in love."

"Wow," he murmured.

"Are you hungry?" Garland inquired. "The food is ready."

Jordin glanced over at Ethan who nodded. "Sure," she responded.

Ethan heard the patter of tiny feet and turned in time to see Kai and her sister.

Kai sidled closer to him, sending him an adoring look beneath a luxurious curl of thick eyelashes. "This is my sister. Her name is Amya."

Ethan smiled. "Hello, Amya. My name is Ethan."

"Hi…" she murmured with a grin. "Kai said you're her friend. I want you to be my friend too."

"I'm friends with your daddy and Jordin. I'll be happy to be your friend as well."

She clapped her hands with glee.

"You gotta be his friend too," Kai instructed her sister.

"I'll be your friend, Mr. Ethan."

"You can just call me Ethan, little lady."

"He's our friend, Daddy," Kai announced, prompting laughter from Ethan.

"You are a very lucky man," he told Ryker.

"I agree."

Ethan felt a prick of sadness at the thought of never being able to settle down with a wife or children. It was something he never really considered—mostly because the only woman he could picture in his life was Jordin. The idea that she wanted more than friendship with him felt surreal. He had never allowed himself to imagine that they could be lovers or anything more.

At the dining room table, Jordin leaned over and whispered, "You look lost in thought."

"I've been thinking about what you said," Ethan stated. "I'm willing to meet with your friend." He was tired of being angry with his parents. Maybe talking this out with a psychologist could help. Ethan was ready to try anything.

"I really believe you should do this," she responded. "I'm sure it'll help."

He met her gaze. "I trust you."

The doorbell rang.

"Are you expecting anyone?" Garland asked her husband.

Ryker rose to his feet. "No."

He excused himself from the table.

Ryker returned a few minutes later with his mother in tow.

Rochelle DuGrandpre stopped in her tracks when she saw Jordin and Ethan. "Oh, I didn't know you had company."

"You would have, had you bothered to call before coming over," Ryker stated.

"Would you like to join us for lunch?" Garland inquired.

Rochelle sent Ryker a sharp glare before responding, "Don't mind if I do."

Rochelle sat down in the empty chair beside Jordin. "Hey, sweetie. Forgive my manners. I didn't mean to be so rude."

"It's good to see you, Aunt Rochelle."

Rochelle glanced over at Ethan and asked, "How is your mother doing?"

"The last time I saw her, she looked fine," he responded before biting into his hamburger.

Silence rang around the room.

"Everything is delicious, honey," Ryker interjected.

Jordin agreed.

Rochelle continued to probe. "I heard she was back in Charleston. I just assumed she returned with you."

Ethan's mouth tightened. "She didn't come with me."

"Why don't we change the subject?" Ryker stated firmly.

Rochelle shrugged. "Just trying to make conversation."

"Grandma, Mr. Ethan is our friend," Kai said.

Amya confirmed what her sister said by nodding.

"Well, isn't that lovely," Rochelle uttered before taking a sip of her iced tea.

"I'm sorry about that," Jordin said when they were alone in the family room after everyone had eaten.

"It's okay. Your aunt hasn't changed at all over the years."

"No, she hasn't. She drives Ryker crazy at times."

"I know that I've never been on her list of favorites," Ethan stated. "She would never let him stay over at my house—I always had to stay with them."

"You weren't the only one she treated like that," Jordin responded. "Aubrie never wanted to bring anybody home because of her mother."

"I guess I'm not the only one with mother issues," he said.

"You're among millions, I'm afraid."

"At least I have you in my corner."

She smiled. "I will always be here for you, Ethan."

Jordin walked out of the kickboxing class, patting her face with a terry-cloth towel, which was damp from the hour-long workout. She broke into a grin when her gaze landed on Ethan.

"How did you enjoy the class?" he asked.

"It was intense, but great," she responded. Jordin dabbed at her neck and chest with the towel. "I always feel good after a rigorous workout. I'm sure tomorrow will be another story."

He chuckled. "You'll be sore. Make sure you do some more stretching later. It'll help."

They walked over to the juice bar and sat down.

"I met with your friend earlier," Ethan announced.

Jordin straightened to relieve the ache in her shoulders. "What do you think?"

"I'm going to see her again next week. We'll see what comes of this."

"Just keep an open mind, Ethan."

"I'm trying to do that."

"What are your plans for this evening?" Ethan asked as they headed to their cars a few minutes later.

"I don't have any plans," she responded.

"I was thinking about having dinner at Aubrie's restaurant. I keep hearing how great it is. Are you interested in joining me?"

The thought thrilled her. She always enjoyed spending time with Ethan. "I'd love to," Jordin responded with a smile.

They were interrupted by one of the staff members needing Ethan's assistance. "I'll call you with the time."

"I'll talk to you later," she told him.

Ethan was very hands-on, but avoided being a micromanager, Jordin noted. He was well respected by his employees and from what she'd heard, he had a reputation of being fair.

She was thrilled that he'd taken her suggestion to see Bree and hoped that this would help free him from his past. Ethan had experienced enough pain—it was now time for him to find his path to happiness. To find his way to the woman who loved him dearly.

Chapter 13

Jordin glanced around the restaurant. Her cousin's eatery was decorated in warm colors of gold and copper tones. "I can't remember the last time I was on a real date. We have been hanging out more than I have in the last couple of years."

Ethan took a sip of his iced tea. "C'mon, I find that hard to believe."

"It's mostly on my part," Jordin admitted. "I've been focused on work."

"Maybe you should take your own advice," he suggested. "You need to get out more and have some fun."

"This is why I spend so much time with you. We have a good time together."

"I'm sure you want something more. Don't you want to get married?"

"Of course I do, but it's still a ways off."

"We both turned out to be workaholics," Ethan said with a chuckle.

Jordin nodded in agreement. "This just means that we have to play hard to balance it all out."

"Only you would say something like this."

She broke into a grin. "Life is short, Ethan. We only get one so we might as well enjoy it every chance we get."

"Do you feel up to coming by the house to see what your mother has done to the place?"

"I've love to see it, Ethan. She's mentioned how much she really enjoyed it. She told me that your house is stunning and it was her favorite project to date."

"She did a fantastic job."

They left the restaurant and drove to his new home.

"I love the verandas on this house," she murmured as they pulled into the driveway.

Inside, Jordin stood in the middle of the living room, trying to take in every angle. The formal dining room, located off the foyer, offered elegant wainscoting, exquisitely designed crown molding and a gorgeous chandelier. "This is beautiful, Ethan."

"I can't take any credit for it. Your mother chose the paint, curtains…everything. All I told her is that I wanted something that would dazzle but inspire my guests to feel at home."

"It's very elegant, but also very welcoming," Jordin stated. "While it looks like it should be in a magazine— it's not so picture-perfect that your guests will be afraid to sit down and relax."

She strolled over to check out the photos on the mantel. "Oh, my goodness," she uttered. "Why do you have this photo of us on your fireplace?"

"It's the only picture I have of us together."

Jordin's gaze met his. "You kept it all this time…"

"Yeah."

Across the hall from the dining room, French doors opened into a study with built-in shelves and double doors opening out to the wraparound front porch.

The bright and spacious kitchen was artfully appointed with top-of-the-line stainless steel appliances.

"Ethan, your home is beautiful."

He smiled. "Thank you."

His cell phone rang.

Ethan glanced down and sighed. "It's Lydia."

"I have to be honest with you, Ethan. I just have a hard time imagining your mother in prison for trafficking drugs. She was always warning us to stay away from marijuana and cocaine. Remember how she would give us articles to read?"

"She's a hypocrite," Ethan stated without emotion.

"Then tell her that," Jordin stated. "Ethan, you didn't ask for my opinion, but I'm giving it anyway. I think you really need to have this conversation with your mom— you need to talk to her and deal with the truth."

"You keep missing the point, Jordin. I don't *want* a relationship with Lydia."

"Do you really believe this is the healthiest way to deal with this situation?" she challenged.

"It's my way."

She gave a slight shrug. "I can't change your mind?"

Ethan shook his head no. "My mother did this to herself."

Jordin could not believe how stubborn he was being about *one* conversation with his mother. She could not imagine his hurt, but to just shut out the very person who gave him life…it was too hard for her to digest.

"It's getting late," she said. "I should probably get going."

"I'll walk you to your car."

Jordin tried not to let it bother her when Ethan did not try to convince her to stay.

Ethan got a chance to see Jordin in court and admired her devotion to family law. She presented her case well, her empathy genuine.

He felt bad over the way he'd left things with her the night before. She glimpsed in his direction; a flash of surprise colored her expression briefly. Jordin had had no idea he would be there to see her. She looked gorgeous in the black-and-red color-blocked suit she was wearing with matching shoes. Her hair was pulled back into a bun, giving her a smooth, professional look.

He could hear the passion in her voice as she talked. She truly loved what she was doing—it was evident in the way she carried herself.

"Wow... I'm impressed," Ethan stated when Jordin walked out of the courtroom an hour later. "You did an outstanding job back there."

"Thank you," she murmured. "I was really shocked to see you in the courtroom."

"I wanted to apologize for last night."

"You don't owe me an apology."

He smiled. "Can I make it up to you tonight?"

Jordin gave a slight shrug. "Sure, if you're up to it."

"I am," he confirmed. "We need to talk."

She scanned his face. "Sounds serious."

He reached over and grabbed her hand. "I owe you a full explanation and I'm ready to talk to you about everything that happened."

"Okay. Instead of going out to dinner, why don't we just stay in?" Jordin suggested. "I'll make something."

"Is seven o'clock okay?"

She nodded. "I'll see you then."

The fact that Ethan was ready to talk made Jordin happy. She did not like the veil of distance that stood between them. Having this conversation just might be the catalyst to propel their relationship to the next level. At least, this was her fervent wish.

After dinner, Ethan and Jordin settled down in her family room to talk.

"I know that you don't understand why I'm so angry with Lydia."

"No, I really don't," she responded. "Ethan, what did your mother do that was so unforgivable?"

"She chose her drug-dealing boyfriend over her son," he responded. "Rob was so possessive of Lydia. He didn't even want her spending time with me. I don't blame him as much as I blame her. She should have sent him on his way." Ethan sighed irritably.

"There's something I want to know. Why didn't you tell me what was really going on? All you told me was that you had to move in with your father," Jordin asked.

"Because I didn't want you running to your parents."

"Why not? They would've helped you, Ethan."

"When my dad came, I thought he wanted to finally be a father to me, but he didn't. He sent me off to military school so I couldn't be a daily reminder to his wife that he cheated on her with Lydia."

"I'm sorry you had to deal with all of this alone."

"Growing up, I really wanted to impress you, Jordin." He paused a heartbeat before adding, "That's why I always tried to put a positive spin on my situation. I was ashamed to tell you that Lydia had gone to prison, but I knew you'd find out somehow."

"Ethan, you had no reason to be ashamed."

"Right…"

"I guess you think I wouldn't have understood because I'm a DuGrandpre."

"Something like that," he admitted.

"I would have been there for you, Ethan."

"That's just it," he pointed out. "I didn't want any-body's pity."

Jordin gave him a sharp look. "You should know me much better than that."

"I realize that now, but back then…"

She reached over and took his hand into her own. "I am so proud of you, Ethan. Despite all that happened to you—look at all you accomplished."

Ethan met her gaze. "I hope that you can try and un-derstand why I choose *not* to have a relationship with the two people who brought me into this world. They haven't been parents to me."

"Your mother wants to have a relationship with you."

He shrugged in nonchalance. "It's too late."

Jordin did not respond. She could feel Ethan's pain.

"I hope that one day you two will be able to sit down together and have a conversation, if only to clear the air."

"I don't know if that day will ever come, Jordin."

"I can keep hoping."

Ethan smiled. "Forever looking for happily-ever-after."

Jordin grinned. "I own it."

"I really don't want to pull you into my craziness."

"I'm here if you need me, Ethan."

His eyes traveled to hers. "Thank you for being such a good friend."

"As your friend, I recommend that we play hooky to-morrow."

"And do what?"

"Whatever we want," Jordin announced. "As long as

it's fun and relaxing. You've been so busy with the gym and the house…let's take a break. I definitely need one and so do you."

Jordin took Ethan to the place they used to frequent as kids where they played arcade games. They walked hand in hand maneuvering around wandering children trying to win tickets to redeem for prizes. Red, yellow, blue and green lights blinked all around them as the sounds of bells, whistles and laughter tickled their ears.

Ethan chose a racing game in the arcade. He and Jordin sat side by side, each one striving to be the top scorer.

Jordin won the first game.

"I see you're still very competitive."

She shrugged. "It's me and I own it."

He laughed.

"Remember how I used to beat you at this game?"

Ethan shook his head no. "I don't remember it that way at all. In fact, this is not the same game."

"It's similar to the one we used to play," she responded. "You're just scared."

He laughed. "Scared? Not me. C'mon, let's get this over with."

Ethan had the highest score the second time around.

"Okay, we have to play one more time," Jordin said. "We can't leave it as a tie."

"You're on."

Jordin competed with fierceness. She stole a peek at Ethan, who looked like he was having the time of his life.

"I win," she stated.

"That's because I'm a little rusty."

"A lot rusty," Jordin corrected with a chuckle.

When they tired of playing, Jordin and Ethan gave all of their tickets to a young girl before leaving the arcade.

"That was so much fun," she said.

He agreed. "I haven't done that in such a long time."

"We should do this at least once a month."

"Sounds like a plan," Ethan responded. "So what's on the agenda next?"

"I was thinking that we could drive down to Battery Park and walk around like we used to do when we were kids."

"Let's go."

"I want you to know that you're not alone, Ethan. We can get through anything you're facing—we can do it together."

He looked at her, his gaze intense.

She was watching him, studying his expression. Jordin smiled then, stirring something within him.

Chapter 14

Saturday morning, Jordin was up early. She had just finished cleaning up when the telephone rang.

"Ethan, hello."

"Hey, I'm in the mood to play tennis," he said. "Want to play?"

She broke into a smile. "Sure."

Jordin hadn't played in a while, but she was not about to let this opportunity to spend time with Ethan pass by. "I have to warn you though. I'm a bit out of practice."

"Just don't put up a fuss when I win."

Her competitive nature took over, prompting her to respond, "I'm not that bad, Ethan."

"I'll see you around nine."

"I'll be ready," Jordin responded.

He arrived to pick her up an hour later.

"You look like you're ready to play," Ethan stated, his

eyes traveling from her face to the white tennis outfit she was wearing. "You look cute."

Jordin held up her racket. "Remember this?"

He laughed. "You still have that old thing?"

She nodded. "Of course. You gave it to me before I found out you were leaving town for good." Jordin met his gaze. "I love this tennis racket because it was all I had of you."

"When I left...I didn't know at the time that I would never be coming back." Ethan turned away from her. "I really didn't want to leave, Jordin."

"I know that you had no choice."

"Back then, I was too immature to understand that my life had been taken away from me. I figured I'd spend some time with my dad but end up back in Charleston. It was my plan."

"Ethan, I understand why you left and didn't come back at that time. I just thought that you would've returned before now—even if it was just for a visit."

"I guess there's no point in looking back," he uttered. "I'm here now."

"Do you regret coming back here?"

"No," Ethan responded. "I had reservations initially, but now...I'm glad to be back." He placed an arm around Jordin. "It's good to be home."

An undeniable magnetism was building between them, forcing Ethan to acknowledge the truth—he could not just ignore the deep feelings he had for Jordin. They were never going to go away.

He was not looking forward to their evening coming to an end. He didn't want to leave her. Ethan enjoyed spending time with her.

"What are you thinking about?"

He glanced over at her. "About you."

Jordin frowned. "What about me?"

"You are incredible."

She smiled. "I think you're pretty incredible yourself."

Ethan found himself wanting to open up to her about his feelings. Instead, he fought the urge.

Jordin studied him for a moment. "What's really going on with you, Ethan?"

He searched for the right words and settled on the truth. "I know it was my decision for us to keep our relationship as just friends, but I'm having some trouble with it."

"So what are you saying?" Jordin inquired.

"You're very special to me. I think you know that."

"Ethan, if you're not feeling me—just let me know," she quickly interjected. "I'm a big girl. I can take it."

"That's not it at all," he responded. "My feelings for you go beyond friendship, Jordin."

"So do mine," she said.

He met her gaze and smiled. "I… What happens now?"

"What do you want to happen, Ethan?"

He chuckled. "That's a loaded question."

Jordin laughed. "Seriously, where do you want to go with this? I know what I want and that's to be with you."

"I want to be with you, sweetheart." He paused a few minutes before adding, "I love you and I'm tired of fighting my feelings."

"I've been waiting for years to hear you say this," Jordin responded softly. "I love you too."

Their eyes met and held.

"Say it again."

She smiled. "I love you, Ethan."

"That's what I needed to hear."

Jordin wrapped her arms around him, pulling him

closer to her. She could feel his uneven breathing on her cheek, as he held her tightly.

Ethan traced his fingertip across her lip causing Jordin's skin to tingle when he touched her. He paused to kiss her, sending currents of desire through her. He kissed her again, pouring into that kiss every emotion and hunger that had hounded him for the past eleven years.

She wrapped her arms around his neck, meeting his passion with her own. The intensity of the fire that bounded up between them threatened to engulf her.

"Make love to me," she whispered between kisses.

"You don't know how badly I've wanted to hear those words come out of your mouth," he confessed. "I've wanted you from the moment I saw you again."

Ethan bent his head and captured her lips in a demanding kiss. Locking her hands behind his neck, Jordin returned his kiss, matching passion for passion.

Her desire soaring, she eased away from him and removed her shirt. Ethan helped her undress. His breath seemed to catch when he glimpsed her in her underwear.

"You are so beautiful," he told her in a husky voice.

Ethan undressed himself and joined her in the bed, his mouth covering hers again hungrily.

Holding her close, he rolled her across the bed and she went with him willingly and eagerly. Moaning, Jordin drew herself closer to him as his hands explored her body.

He slipped on a condom to protect them both.

Jordin offered him her lips once more while offering Ethan her body as well, entangling her legs with his.

Jordin hummed softly as she walked toward her office the next day. Her sister was in the hallway talking to Austin.

"Good morning, siblings."

Jadin surveyed her face. "Why are you so happy this morning?"

"It's a beautiful day."

"Naaah…it's more than that."

Austin agreed. "Anything you need to tell us?"

Jordin smiled. "No, not really."

They followed her into her office.

She sank down in her chair, asking, "Why are you two following me? There's nothing to tell."

"Liar…" Jadin uttered.

"What she said," Austin stated. "I told you that you wear your feelings on your face."

Her brother was right. Jordin decided it was best to tell them or she would never be able to get any work done.

"Okay… Ethan and I are officially dating," she announced. "We love each other and we're finally ready to move forward."

"It certainly took him long enough," Jadin stated.

"I love him so much."

"I know," Austin and Jadin said in unison.

"Oh, and we did notice your glow, but I prefer not to discuss it." Austin headed to the door. "Congratulations."

Jadin stayed behind. "So was it all you dreamed it would be?"

Jordin broke into a grin. "He is truly the other part of my being."

"I know I've had my doubts, but I'm happy for you, sis. I know you've dreamed of being with Ethan since we were teens. I'm glad it's worked out for you."

"Thanks."

"I'm at the courthouse most of the morning, but do you want to get together for lunch?"

"Sure," Jordin responded. "I'll meet you over there."

She watched her sister leave before turning on her computer.

Jordin could not help smiling as she recalled the events of the night before. Making love to Ethan was everything she'd dreamed of and more. Her eyes grew wet at the memory of Ethan declaring his love for her. She loved him so much that it defied reason.

Jadin entered the office carrying a bouquet of red roses. "These just came for you."

He sent me flowers, she thought with a smile. "They're beautiful."

Her sister agreed. "They smell heavenly too."

Jordin made space for the vase on her desk. "Ethan is such a sweetheart." She glanced over at her sister. "It can only get better from here."

Ethan was in such a good mood, a few of his employees commented on it. The truth was that it had been a long time since he'd been this happy. A lot of it had to do with Jordin. He did not regret telling her the truth, which was that he had fallen in love with Jordin the very first time he saw her all those years ago. It was freeing to be able to share his true feelings with her.

They were officially a couple now.

He was finally able to envision a future with the only woman he'd ever loved. It was the beginning of a new life—one he had longed for but was afraid would never come to pass.

The phone rang.

"Ethan Holbrooke speaking," he said in greeting.

"Thank you for the roses."

He smiled. "I hope they were the perfect color."

Jordin chuckled. "You can never go wrong with red. They are beautiful and in full bloom."

"I want to see you tonight," Ethan stated.

"That's great," she responded, "because I want to see you too."

"My house or yours?"

"I'll come to you," Jordin replied. "We can pick up dinner from one of the nearby restaurants."

"Sounds like a plan. Oh, and you might want to bring an overnight bag. I'm just saying."

She laughed. "I'll think about it."

They ended the call a few minutes later.

Ethan returned his attention to the mountain of work on his desk. Much of it was most likely invoices. He would go through them before sending them over to accounting.

Later that evening, Jordin showed up at his house around seven. She had already picked up dinner for them.

"I keep thinking about your mom," she said as they settled down at the dining room table.

He did not respond.

Jordin placed a napkin in her lap. "Ethan…"

"What do you want me to say?"

"Aren't you at least worried about her?"

Ethan shook his head. "Why should I be? She's fine."

"I know that you don't want to have anything to do with her, but do you know what's going on with her? Where she lives or where she is working? That doesn't bother you?"

"I know that she is staying with a friend of hers, Jordin. I guess she has a job doing something. What do you want me to do?" Ethan wiped his mouth on a napkin.

Jordin reached over and covered his hand with her own. "I think you should make sure that she is fine— she's your mother…"

He sliced off a piece of chicken and stuck it in his mouth, chewing slowly.

Jordin let the subject of Lydia die as they finished their meal. She hated this distance between Ethan and his mother.

She tried to bring the topic up once more after they got settled on the couch, but Ethan interjected, "I don't want to spend our time discussing Lydia. Instead I'd rather be kissing you."

Her eyes strayed to his lips.

"We've been talking about her for almost an hour now. I don't know about you, but I'm sure we could be doing something much more enjoyable."

Jordin made a small gasping sound when his mouth drifted across hers. "Isn't this better?"

He pulled away and looked down at her, as if expecting her to protest. When she did not, Ethan reclaimed her lips, deepening the kiss.

He hungered for the feel of her lips against his. Kissing Jordin was like adding oxygen to a fire that had been smoldering, unseen for years. The heat had overcome the ice and was soon a blazing wildfire.

His desire for her took over, and Ethan led her to the bedroom, all thoughts of his mother dissipated as they removed their clothes and climbed into bed. All that existed was skin-on-skin contact, the soft sighs of their heightened breathing, heartbeats thundering in a raging sea of desire. Each breath they took became a sigh sifting into the quiet.

Chapter 15

"What's this?" Jordin asked when Ethan handed her an odd-shaped gift the next morning after breakfast. They had been dating for a couple of months and things between them were great.

"Open it," he prompted.

"It's a tennis racket."

"I wanted to get you a new one," Ethan stated. "You took really good care of my old one, but I think it's time you had a much nicer racket."

She smiled. "Thank you, Ethan. This is really sweet."

He kissed her. "These past three months have been so amazing with you. I can't remember being so happy."

Smiling, Jordin murmured, "Same here."

"I'm crazy about you, babe."

She touched her lips to his. "I can't put into words how much I love you, Ethan."

The telephone rang.

He glanced at the number, but did not answer.

"Is that your mother?"

"No. It's been a while since I've heard anything from her. That was a toll-free number. I figured it was a tele-marketer."

Although Jordin did not completely agree with Ethan on the subject of his mother, she had to admit that he was in a much better frame of mind since he started seeing Bree. It helped that Lydia had not been calling or sending letters.

Since they started dating, Ethan was much more relaxed as well. They spent a lot of time together when he was not traveling.

"Are you in the mood to try out your new racket?" he asked.

"Maybe later," Jordin stated. "Right now, I just want to cuddle with you on this incredibly comfortable couch and watch TV with you."

"I'm warning you if we cuddle, we may not leave this house at all."

She grinned. "That's fine with me."

Jordin clutched at him, pressing close even as Ethan pulled her closer still.

It wasn't enough for either of them.

"I love you so much," he managed between breaths.

Jordin's body was still on fire and humming with sensation from their last lovemaking session. Heart racing, breath ragged, she couldn't think of anything other than physically connecting with her soul mate.

"Let's go to the bedroom," Ethan whispered.

Replete from another round of lovemaking, Ethan held Jordin captive in his arms.

"What are you thinking about?" she whispered.

"You," he responded. "I never thought I could love someone as much as I love you, sweetheart. You own my soul."

"I know," she responded tenderly. "When you make love to me, it's with deep emotion. What you don't say with your mouth—you tell me with your body."

"We've come a long way to get to this point. All this time…"

"Wasted," Jordin finished for him. "But that's all over. You've finally come to your senses."

He chuckled.

She turned in his arms, facing him.

"No more talking," Jordin whispered sleepily. "I just want to savor this moment."

She was sleeping soundly a few minutes later.

When Jordin woke up, she found herself in bed all alone. She called out for Ethan, but received no response.

She glanced at her phone. There was a text from him.

Went to grab something for us to eat. Luv you much.

Jordin swung her legs out of bed. She padded naked into the bathroom to take a shower.

She was dressed in jeans and tank top by the time Ethan returned with food.

He smiled. "I thought you'd still be sleeping."

"Maybe if you were still in bed with me," she responded. "I missed you."

Ethan kissed her. "I'm here now."

She sniffed. "Something smells delicious."

"I picked up some barbecue chicken, macaroni and cheese, turnip greens and fresh baked bread."

"Ooooh," she said.

"I figured I'd grab this since we will probably eat a really late dinner."

"This is pretty much all I'll need," Jordin said.

They sat down at the table to eat.

"My parents invited us over on Sunday," Jordin announced. "Do you want to go?"

"Is your aunt going to be there?"

"She might."

Ethan shook his head no. "I think I'll pass."

"Don't let Aunt Rochelle get to you," Jordin said.

"She's a little more than I really want to deal with right now," Ethan confessed. "I especially don't want her questioning me about my mother."

Jordin nodded in understanding. "I get it."

"You're not disappointed, are you?"

"No," she responded. "I've been wanting to spend time with the girls, so it's perfect."

Ethan smiled. "Give Kai and Amya a hug from me."

"You know you've been upgraded to best-friend status."

He laughed. "What did I do to deserve that?"

"Gifts from the Disney Store and ice cream," Jordin reminded him. "Then there was the day at the movies and dinner after."

"You planned all those things."

"But *you* were there. I think they just adore you."

He met her gaze. "Jealous?"

"No, I think it's cute. Besides, I'm the only woman for you."

"That you are," Ethan confirmed. "I've never met anyone to make me feel what you do. There was a time when I wanted to forget you, but I could not. You kept popping into my mind."

"I've never been one to take no for an answer," she said with a grin.

Laughing, he agreed.

Chapter 16

"Do you have any plans for the weekend after next?" Ethan inquired a few days later when they walked out of the movie theater.

Jordin shook her head no. "What's up?"

"I was thinking that we could use a few days away from Charleston. We could take a long weekend and go somewhere romantic."

She broke into a smile. "Sounds wonderful."

"Anyplace special you'd like to go?" he asked.

She gave him a sidelong glance. "Why don't you surprise me, Ethan?"

His brows rose in surprise. "You would just up and go with me like that?"

Jordin nodded. "I trust you, Ethan. I know that you wouldn't do anything crazy."

Ethan chuckled. "Hmmmm... Maybe I'll take you to Utah or Montana. We can go work a ranch or something."

She paused in her tracks. "I don't think so. For the record, I would like to go somewhere tropical—not a dude ranch."

"Montana has some cool ranches."

"Not interested," Jordin murmured.

"You're sure?"

She nodded. "I'm positive, Ethan. I don't want anything to do with horses, cows, sheep…anything close to that."

He wrapped an arm around her. "Okay, we'll go someplace tropical."

They walked to his car.

Ethan opened the door to the passenger side for Jordin.

He walked around to the other side of the vehicle and got in. "Are we going back to your place or mine?"

"I'm working from home tomorrow," Jordin announced, "so why don't we stay at my house?" She could not wipe the grin off her face. She was blissfully happy. She and Ethan were closer than ever—things were perfect.

After their walk along the sandy shoreline, she and Ethan sat down on a huge beach towel that he had pulled out of the trunk of his car, talking as they watched the waves tossing back and forth.

He'd surprised her with a trip to Martinique in the French West Indies. Jordin loved everything about the island…the food, the culture and the scenery. That was not Ethan's only surprise. He owned the house they were currently staying in—she did not find out until they arrived.

"What would you like to talk about now?" Jordin asked.

"How about this?" Ethan leaned forward and kissed her. His kiss was slow, thoughtful and sent spirals of de-

sire racing through Jordin. "Mmmm… I love the subject matter."

"Why don't we head back to the house?" Ethan suggested. "I know that you're cold."

"Thank you," she said with a chuckle.

They left the beach and went back to his home.

Jordin loved the design of Ethan's house and the amazing ocean, mountain and city-lights views from every
room. He had given her a tour of the five-bedroom house
with fabulous West Indies decor throughout.

From where she was standing, she had a fantastic view
of the colorful flower garden, the ocean and the sprawl-
ing deck out back. Ethan was having an outdoor kitchen
installed. Grilling was one of his favorite pastimes.

Jordin turned away from the window.

This area is so beautiful, she thought. Her eyes traveled from the faux-finished stucco walls to the hand-
painted furniture to the huge overstuffed sofas. She'd
asked him why he had so many bedrooms and Ethan responded that they came with the house. Then he'd told
her that he wanted to marry and settle down, so he kept
that in mind while he was searching for a home.

She glanced down at the marbled floor throughout the
first level. Jordin loved hardwoods, but she had to admit
Ethan's flooring was nice.

Ethan walked into the bedroom that evening shortly
after nine o'clock. He had been in the living room checking voice mail messages while Jordin showered. She was
sitting in bed reading a book with the pillows propped
behind her back.

He slid in beside her and laced his fingers through her
curls, before leaning closer to the warm skin of her neck
to trace a pattern of kisses to her jawline. "What are you
reading?" he whispered against her cheek.

"Ummm..." Jordin's thoughts were no longer on the book in her hands.

"I guess it's not that interesting," Ethan stated as he reached over and closed her book, then put it on the nightstand on her side of the bed.

"It's not," she responded softly.

"You have no idea how long I've wanted to spend time with you in a romantic setting."

Jordin met his gaze. "This place is perfect and being here with you, Ethan... It feels right."

He kissed her softly on her lips. "There has never been any other woman for me—not one who makes me feel the way you do." When he held her, she felt like no other female. It felt like Jordin was made for him, made to fit him like a glove. Ethan could not seem to get close enough to her.

"I feel the same way about you."

Ethan pulled the covers up over them and wrapped her in his arms and legs, snuggling closer to her as they lay together in bed. He kissed her lips in a tantalizing slow kiss.

She drew away from him. "Did I ever tell you that you're a great kisser?"

"So are you," Ethan responded with a grin.

"I'm so happy."

He smiled. "So am I."

"How often do you come to Martinique?" Jordin inquired.

"Two to three times a year. I love this island. That's why I decided to buy this place."

Her eyes traveled the room. "You put so much into this house...were you planning to live here permanently at some point?"

"Yes," Ethan admitted. "I considered that this is where I'd like to live out my retirement."

She looked at him. "Is this still your plan?"

"Not really," Ethan replied. "I'm not going to leave you in Charleston and I don't expect you to give up your job. This will be our vacation home."

She loved the idea of a vacation home with Ethan as she hoped to spend the rest of her life with him. They had not discussed marriage, but Jordin felt that the topic could come up at any time. She was ready to settle down for marriage and a family. Jordin believed that she and Ethan were on the same page when it came to taking their relationship to the next level, but she did not know if he was ready for marriage.

Jordin closed her eyes as she let her body sink into his. She knew she would never be happy with another man if her time with Ethan ever ran out.

They were going to do some sightseeing and shopping around noon. She was so comfortable in Ethan's arms that she did not want the moment to end. "Why don't we just stay here and watch movies?" she suggested.

He planted a kiss on her forehead. "Seriously?"

"I love it here in your arms. I feel safe and secure. I just don't want to give this up right now. I love this feeling."

"Why don't we go on and get the shopping out of the way. We can have an early dinner and come back here to relax for the rest of the evening."

"That sounds nice," she murmured.

"Let's get going, sweetheart."

Jordin rose to her feet and went to slip on her shoes. She was enjoying her time on this exotic island with the man she loved. He seemed much more relaxed in this space, which made her wonder if Lydia continued to be a source of discomfort to him. He was still seeing Bree and Jordin did not ask him to disclose his conversations with the therapist.

His happiness mattered to her, but Jordin still believed that he would not be completely free until he found a way to forgive his mother.

Chapter 17

Jordin chose a silky purple dress with an A-line skirt that flared just around her knees. Swarovski crystals sprinkled like raindrops from the shoulder to the waist. Wearing it made her feel very sexy, especially with the strappy high-heel silver sandals.

"Are you sure this place is open?" she asked, observing her surroundings. "There aren't any cars in the parking lot. I don't think this is a good sign."

"The parking lot's empty because I booked the restaurant just for us."

Jordin paused in her steps. "You shut down this place for the two of us? Why?"

Ethan nodded. "I want this to be a special night for us."

She wondered briefly what he had in mind for the evening, but she was not concerned. Every moment on this island had been special as far as Jordin was concerned. She was thrilled that some of the old Ethan had returned during their time together. He was not as tense as he usually was when they were in Charleston.

Jordin and Ethan were seated immediately after entering the upscale restaurant. They had barely sat down when waiters appeared out of nowhere, bringing in trays of food as soft jazz floated around the room.

They enjoyed a five-star dinner with crystal-blue water and bright stars as their backdrop.

"I could stay here forever," Jordin murmured.

Ethan smiled. "Really? You'd leave Charleston?"

She was quiet for a moment before saying, "If I was ready to give up my job, but until then, I think we should come here as often as we can." Jordin took a sip of her wine, before adding, "Look at me, I'm taking over your place."

"I'm glad you feel at home here," Ethan said.

"I really do," she confirmed.

"Jordin, I wanted tonight to be special because there's something I want to ask you." Ethan took a small box out of his pocket and opened it to reveal an elegant diamond ring in a platinum setting. The stone was an emerald-cut diamond surrounded by smaller princess-cut diamonds.

Her eyes filled with tears. "Oh, wow…wow…that's gorgeous…"

"Will you marry me?"

Jordin gasped as Ethan gently placed it on her finger.

She looked up at him, her surprise evident on her face. "I never expected this."

"I love you, Jordin," he said softly. "I want to spend the rest of my life with you…if you'll have me."

"Yes… YES," she responded. "All those years you were gone—it felt like a part of me was missing. I don't want to feel that way ever again, Ethan. I love you."

"I guess this means that we're getting married."

"This is definitely what it means," she responded with a grin. Jordin glanced down at the ring on her finger and murmured, "It's so beautiful."

"I'm glad you like it."

When they returned to the house there was a bottle of champagne on ice and a plate laden with assorted cheese, crackers and white-chocolate-dipped strawberries.

"Did you arrange this too?"

"I did," Ethan responded. "The night isn't over."

He spun her to face him and began to string searing kisses across her shoulders and up her neck.

A moan escaped from her lips and Jordin felt her legs go weak.

He lifted her and carried her to the bed. Ethan laid her down on her back and stretched out next to her.

"You are so incredibly stunning, sweetheart," he murmured. "You take my breath away."

Ethan woke with Jordin in his arms feeling better than he had in a long time. He felt a deep sense of peace for the first time since returning home. He stared at his sleeping fiancée and smiled.

She is so beautiful.

Jordin released a soft moan as she snuggled against him.

He kissed her. "Wake up, beautiful."

She stretched in his arms and smiled up at him. "Good morning."

Ethan could not help but wonder at the way she made him feel, at the intensity of his feelings for her. "Morning."

She sat up in bed and stared down at her ring finger. "So it wasn't a dream."

He grinned. "No, we're very much engaged."

"This is a dream come true for me. You're the only man I ever thought I'd marry."

"I bought the house with the idea that we would live in it as husband and wife, but I wasn't sure if that would really happen," Ethan confessed, "but it looks like I'm getting my greatest wish."

Jordin pulled his face to hers, kissing him. "I love you, Ethan Holbrooke."

"I love you too."

"Shower?" she asked with a smile.

Ethan broke into a grin. "I'll go start the water."

"I'll join you in a few minutes," Jordin responded.

He slipped out of bed and crossed the room toward the bathroom.

She watched him as he padded barefoot, taking in the tight muscles in his legs and the bands of muscles crisscrossing his back. Everything about Ethan was perfection.

"I'm a lucky girl," she whispered.

Ethan called out to her a moment later that the water was ready. She slipped into the bathroom and joined him under the hot jets.

Jordin enjoyed the long, slow and wet shower with the man she loved. They were leaving for Charleston in the morning—it was time to go back to their lives, but the time they spent in Martinique was perfect. His proposal of marriage had put her over the moon. Things would only get better from this point forward. She looked forward to spending the rest of her life with Ethan.

"How was your vacation?" Austin inquired when Jordin walked into the break room on Monday morning.

"It was perfect," she responded with a smile. "It was the most romantic trip I've ever taken."

"The way you're grinning, something special must have happened. Hold out your hand and let me see it."

"Austin, you're ruining the surprise."

He chuckled. "Your glow is very telling."

Jordin showed him her engagement ring.

"Wow…" he murmured. "Very nice. I'm happy for you."

They embraced.

"Can I have some sibling love?" Jadin uttered from the doorway. "How come I wasn't invited to the party?"

Austin hugged her. "Jordin has some news she wants to share."

Jadin turned to her twin. "What is it?"

"I'm getting married."

"Ethan proposed?"

Jordin held up her hand and nodded. "He asked me to marry him our last night on the island. It was very romantic."

"You and Ethan… I didn't know it had gotten so serious."

"We love each other, Jadin. We want to take our relationship to the next level. I thought you'd be happy for me."

Austin picked up his coffee mug and said, "I'll give you two some privacy."

"I'm walking out with you," Jordin stated. "I'm not going to let *anyone* ruin this day for me."

"What's that all about?" her brother inquired.

"Jadin doesn't think Ethan is the perfect man for me. He doesn't come from a royal bloodline, so to speak."

Austin's eyebrows rose in surprise. "Really?"

"I love her, but our sister can be a bit of a snob. I don't think she would've given Michael a chance if his great-grandfather wasn't the founder of Charleston's oldest African American newspaper."

"Well, from the looks of that ring, Ethan is doing quite well for himself."

"All that matters to me is that he loves me as much as I love him, Austin. Marrying well does not ensure a happy marriage."

Her brother nodded in agreement. "I'm happy for you."

Jordin looked up at him and smiled. "Thanks."

"Can we talk for a moment?" Jadin asked from the doorway an hour later.

Jordin put her guard up and prepared to defend her engagement to Ethan. "Sure."

Jadin closed the door behind her. "I'm sorry about the way I reacted this morning. I was just surprised by the news."

"Why are you so surprised?" Jordin asked. "You have always known about my feelings for Ethan?"

"You can't deny that you two are from very different worlds."

Jordin eyed her twin. "Meaning what? In the African American community, Michael is considered Charleston royalty and you let him go off to California just like that—you say you love him, but I don't think you really do. Ethan didn't grow up with all of the privileges we had, but I don't care. I'm with Ethan because I *love* him in a way that defies definition."

"I just want you to be happy, sis."

"I *am* happy, Jadin," she assured her. "I'm very happy."

"Then I'm thrilled for you. Congratulations."

Jordin was not sure her sister's well-wishes were sincere, but chose not to dwell on the negativity. "Thank you, Jadin."

"When do you plan to tell the rest of the family?"

"Tonight at dinner. Ethan and I are going to tell them together."

"Then you may want to take that ring off your finger."

Chapter 18

"Looks like your entire family is here tonight," Ethan observed aloud when they arrived at her parents' house. "There are a lot of cars here. Looks like a luxury car lot."

"I wanted the whole family together when we made our announcement. I did tell Austin and Jadin earlier but they were sworn to secrecy."

"How do you think your parents are going to take it?" he asked.

"I'm sure they'll be happy for us." As soon as they walked into the house, Jordin stated loudly, "Everyone, I have an announcement to make." When she had everyone's attention, she continued. "Ethan asked me to marry him and I said yes. We're engaged."

There was applause all around the living room, although her father looked surprised by the news.

Jordin followed her father into his office.

Closing the door behind her, she asked, "You didn't

seem truly happy for me when I announced that I was marrying Ethan. Do you have a problem with him, Dad?"

"I like Ethan, but I never considered your relationship with him would go beyond friendship."

"He's a good man, Daddy, and I love him."

"I can see how happy he makes you," Etienne stated. "I have always liked Ethan, despite the rumors about his mother and her boyfriend."

"He had no control over his mother's actions."

"I know this."

"Dad, I want your blessing, but I'm going to marry Ethan no matter what. He is the man for me."

"You are stubborn just like your mother."

Jordin broke into a grin. "It's one of the reasons why you love her."

Etienne gave a slight nod. "True."

"Oh, just so you know… Ethan came to me before you all left on vacation and asked my blessing."

"So why did you look so surprised when I made the announcement?" she asked.

"I guess I wasn't quite ready for the reality of it."

"Dad, are you happy for me?"

He smiled. "Knowing that you are happy fills me with joy, sweetheart. Congratulations."

Jordin and her father walked back to join everyone hand in hand. She was thrilled that she had his approval, although she would have married Ethan regardless.

She walked over to Ethan and smiled.

"Everything okay?" he asked.

Jordin nodded as she sat down beside him.

Ethan was staring at her, sending a delicious shudder through her body.

"What is it?" Jordin asked. "Why are you staring at me like this?"

"I can't get over how beautiful you are," he said, bringing a smile to her lips.

Ethan stroked her face gently.

She glanced around the room to see if any of her family members were watching them. "You do know that we're not alone, Ethan."

"I don't care," he responded. "You are going to be my wife and I hope you won't make me wait too long."

"It depends on the type of wedding you want."

"Actually, that depends on what you prefer, sweetheart. I'd marry you tomorrow if you'd agree."

Jordin smiled. "I'd love to just go to the justice of the peace and get married or elope, but my mother would kill me."

Ryker and his family arrived.

Kai and Amya ran straight to Ethan.

Jordin laughed, as they each had to give him a hug. "The girls adore you, Ethan."

He smiled. "They are cuties."

"I like watching you with them," Jordin confessed when they went into the kitchen with Garland. "You will make a great father one day."

Ethan shook his head no. "I don't want to be a father. My mother and father were terrible examples of parenthood."

His words stunned her. "The actions of your parents don't mean that you will be a bad parent."

He shrugged in nonchalance. "It's a decision I made long ago."

Ethan not wanting children was something that had never occurred to Jordin. In fact, it came as a complete shock and could possibly change everything between them.

Pain twisted with misery became a tangled mess deep inside her. Jordin swallowed hard.

She stole a glance at Ethan before saying, "I'm going to see if I can help Garland." She needed some time to brace herself for whatever happened next.

Chapter 19

It was raining by the time, Jordin and Ethan departed for home.

Clutching her sweater closed, she shivered.

Outside, the wind shrieked, the rain poured and she knew the minute she ventured out of the car, the downpour would soak her clothing to the bone.

"Why are you so quiet?" he asked. "You hardly said a word since we left your parent's house."

"No," she responded. "The weather is nasty, so let's just head back to my place."

"Is everything okay?"

Jordin nodded. She needed some time to digest Ethan's decision to not have children. At some point, they would have to have a discussion, but Jordin was not ready for this conversation tonight.

"Okay, I know something's going on," Ethan uttered. "Did I do something to upset you?"

"I'm just tired," she stated. Jordin fought back tears as they neared her neighborhood. She didn't want Ethan to know how much his words saddened her.

"Is this about my saying that I didn't want children?"

Jordin glanced over at him. "You were being honest and I appreciate that."

"But it bothers you."

"It does," she admitted. "Ethan, it's not something I want to talk about tonight. Can we table this discussion for another day?"

Ethan parked the car in her driveway. "We need to go on and clear the air."

She shook her head. "Not tonight. I just want to take a day or so to think about this."

"Do you want me to come in?"

She gave him a tiny smile. "I don't think I'd be very good company."

"Jordin, I love you like crazy. I didn't have any parental role models. Watching this man and that man coming into my mother's life and treating her bad...my dad... I don't want to bring a child into this world just to fail them."

"We'll talk in a day or so," she responded softly. Jordin wasn't sure she could go through with the marriage, but decided that she was too emotional on the subject of children at the moment to make such a decision.

"This is not the way I wanted this evening to end," Ethan stated.

"This isn't about *want*," Jordin said quietly. "This is about need. Right now, I really need you to leave."

Ethan looked as if he wanted to argue.

"Fine," he said at last. "I'll check on you tomorrow."

She took a deep breath and held it for a moment.

"We will find a way to work this out," Ethan stated.

"Now that you're in my life—I'm not going to lose you like this."

When she was alone in the house, Jordin sank down on the sofa in tears. She loved Ethan so much, but she also wanted to be a mother. She couldn't see her life without children, even with him.

Is this a sign that I shouldn't marry Ethan?

The thought made her feel worse.

The next day, Ethan picked up the telephone to call Jordin, but changed his mind.

She needs time to think and it's best that I give her that time.

He regretted not having discussed children before he proposed. It had not occurred to him that she might want to be a mother one day. He supposed that she wanted to focus on her career while he managed his gyms.

The thought that he might lose her over this disturbed Ethan to the point that he decided to call Jordin. He wanted to convince her of his love and devotion, but would that be enough?

"Hello, Ethan," she said warmly into the receiver.

He smiled. "Babe, I hope you can have lunch with me today. I really want to see you."

"What time did you have in mind?"

"I can be there in about ten minutes."

"Okay," she responded after a brief pause. "I'll see you then."

Jordin pasted on a smile when Ethan entered her office twenty minutes later.

"I ran into your father in the elevator and he walked me past the receptionist."

She rose to her feet. "I'll be ready to leave in about a minute."

During the ride to the restaurant, Jordin had little to say.

"I hate this tension between us," Ethan stated.

"I just don't know what to say right now."

Once they were seated, he said, "I love you more than anything, sweetheart."

"I know that, Ethan," she responded softly. "Love isn't the problem."

"I realize that we should have had this discussion before I proposed to you."

Jordin nodded in agreement. "Now is just as good a time as any. We're not married yet."

"Is this going to be a deal breaker for you?" Ethan wanted to know.

"I'm not sure," Jordin responded. "I want to be a mother and apparently this is a giant problem for you."

He pointed to her menu. "Do you know what you want to eat?"

"Ethan, I'm not really hungry."

"I can see this is really upsetting for you."

"It is," Jordin confessed. "I never once considered that we would have opposing views on children."

Jordin's eyes watered.

Ethan reached over and took her hand in his. He didn't know what to say to make her pain go away.

"I'm really not hungry. I'd rather leave and go back to my office, if you don't mind."

"Okay."

He spoke with the waiter, then followed Jordin out of the restaurant and to the car.

Back at the firm, Ethan joined her in her office.

"I don't want to lose you."

"I don't want to lose you either," she responded.

"But do you think that I am enough for you?" he asked. "I need to know."

Before Jordin could respond, a little girl ran into her office, cutting off further conversation between them.

"Hailey, how are you?" she greeted.

Ethan noted the way Jordin's face lit up upon seeing the little girl.

"I'm so sorry," a woman said as she rushed inside. "Hailey, honey, you can't just interrupt Miss DuGrandpre's meeting."

"It's fine. Sherry, this is my fiancé, Ethan."

"Oh, I'm so happy for you. Congratulations."

Ethan sat down on the leather couch in her office while the two women talked. Hailey eyed him with curiosity for a moment before awarding him a tiny wave.

"I can see how much you love children," he said when they were alone.

She nodded. "Yes, I love them very much."

"I know that I said I didn't want children, but after watching you with Ryker's children and now this little girl... I realize that I can't deprive you of being a mother."

Jordin stiffened. "So what are you saying?"

"I don't want to rush into anything, but I think I have to reconsider my decision about being a parent."

"Are you seriously thinking about this?"

He nodded. "I love you and it's obvious that you'd be a great mother, Jordin."

"I want that, Ethan, but I'm not in a hurry. I want to enjoy being husband and wife for a while. If you mean it, then we will decide when it's time to have a child."

"You make me want to be a better man." He loved seeing her happy. Ethan also realized that he had to put his own selfish needs to the side for the woman he loved.

"I just had to get you to see what I already knew— that we're better together," Jordin responded with a grin.

"I really don't want to lose you, so we will have children. I promise I won't make you wait too long."

"I know you won't," she assured him.

He kissed her passionately.

Chapter 20

Ethan glared at his ringing office phone, growled when he saw his mother's name flash across the screen and ignored it. He had not heard from her in a couple of months so he'd assumed that she had given up.

He released a short sigh of relief when it was silent once more. Glancing about his office, Ethan was thankful the marketing team had already left. He wanted some time alone to consider his change of heart regarding parenting.

Jordin deserves to be a mother, but how will I be as a father? Ethan thought about his mother. *This woman just won't leave me alone. I don't want a child of mine to feel the way I feel about Lydia.*

He shook away his thoughts. Ethan knew deep down that he would never treat his child the way he was treated by his parents.

"Are you still at the office?" Jordin asked as soon as he answered his cell phone.

"I'll be leaving in about fifteen minutes," Ethan responded. "Where are you?"

"I'm at home. I just wanted to make sure you were going to be there by the time I arrive."

"You have a key, Jordin. Just let yourself in."

"Okay, I'll see you when you get there."

"Love you, babe," he murmured.

"I love you too."

Ethan was all smiles at the idea of Jordin waiting for him at the house. He was looking forward to spending the evening with her.

Twenty minutes later, he left his office.

As soon as he stepped outside the building, he spotted a woman. Ethan's mood shifted quickly to anger. "What are you doing here, Lydia?"

"I need to talk to you, son."

"You don't have the right to call me that."

"If you'd just give me the chance to talk to you, I can explain everything."

"And say what, Lydia?"

Tears glistened in her eyes. "I'm sorry for not being a good mother to you. You deserved so much better."

"I agree," he uttered. "I did deserve better."

"It's not what you think, Ethan."

"You know I can still remember how many times you lectured about choosing the right friends, about staying away from drugs…" Ethan shook his head in dismay. "You are nothing but a hypocrite."

"I swear to you that I never touched drugs."

"Congratulations," he responded drily.

"Ethan, I realized a long time ago that I made a huge

mistake in dating Rob. He was not the man I thought he was."

"I bet you came to that realization in prison, right?"

"Will you please give me another chance, sweetheart? I miss you so much."

"Now you know how I felt all those years."

"If I could take it all back—I would."

"There are no do-overs, Lydia. Now if you will excuse me, I need to get going."

"I won't keep you."

Ethan walked to his car and unlocked the door.

Despite his feelings for her, he could not just leave her alone downtown like this. "Where are you staying?"

"I'm staying with Trudy. You remember her, don't you?"

He nodded. "Is she still staying in the same place?"

"Yes," Lydia responded. "She's been kind enough to let me stay with her until I can get on my feet."

"Get in and I'll drive you there."

Her eyebrows rose in surprise. "Thank you, Ethan."

"Do you have any money?"

Lydia shook her head no. "I've been trying but I haven't been able to find steady work."

Ethan pulled out his wallet and removed five twenties and a hundred-dollar bill. "Here is two hundred dollars."

"I don't want your money," she responded. "That's not why I came."

Her response surprised him. "Take it, Lydia. You can't be out here without money."

She accepted it. "I'll find a way to pay you back."

"It's not a loan," Ethan explained. "I'm just not heartless enough to see the woman who gave birth to me without a dollar to her name."

"I really appreciate the ride and the money, but mostly

I am grateful that you care about me just a little. It gives me hope that I haven't lost you forever."

Ethan did not respond.

When they arrived, he told Lydia, "I'm going to write you a check. This should help you while you look for work."

"No," she quickly interjected. "I would rather starve than take that check, Ethan. I don't want your money—I want your love and your forgiveness. If you can't give me that..." A lone tear rolled down her cheek. "Thank you for the ride. I won't bother you anymore."

Lydia turned to give him the money back, but he refused, saying, "Keep it. You need some cash."

"What I need is my son."

"Lydia, I wish you well. This is as much as I can offer you right now."

"Did you get caught up in traffic?" Jordin asked when Ethan walked through the front door of his house.

"I dropped Lydia off at her friend's house," he announced. "She was outside my building when I walked out."

"So you had a chance to talk to her then?"

"A little. I'm not ready for a full conversation with Lydia just yet."

"This is the first step in the right direction," Jordin stated.

"I knew you'd say that."

She walked over to him and placed a kiss on his lips. "I'm so proud of you."

"What smells so delicious?" he asked.

"I made a roast for dinner."

"This night is just getting better and better," Ethan murmured against her cheek.

"Wait until you find out what's for dessert."

"What is it?"

Jordin whispered in his ear.

"Let's start with dessert…" Ethan picked her up and carried her up the stairs.

"What about the roast?"

"Is the oven turned off?"

"Yes."

"It can wait."

Jordin held on to him, smiling all the way to the bedroom.

Jordin did not leave for lunch until shortly after two in the afternoon, which was late for her. She left the courthouse later than she'd planned. On the way to her car, she heard someone call out her name.

She glanced around, seeing no familiar face.

"Jordin…"

She turned around once more, this time her gaze landing on a thin woman standing a few feet away. Her hair was a salt-and-pepper color; she was much thinner now and her shoulders looked like they bore the weight of the world, but Jordin recognized her. "Mrs. Holbrooke, how are you?" This was the last person she expected to see.

Lydia looked her up and down. "My goodness, you have grown into such a beautiful woman. It's so nice to see you again."

"Thank you," Jordin responded. "I heard you were back in Charleston."

"You must have talked to Ethan."

She nodded. "Yes, ma'am."

"How is he doing?"

Jordin didn't miss the shimmer of sadness that shone in Lydia's eyes. "He's fine, Mrs. Holbrooke."

"I guess you know that I've been trying to get him to talk to me but he refuses. I know that Ethan's very angry with me." She released a short sigh in resignation. "All I want is a chance to explain everything to him."

"I'm on my way to grab a bite to eat," Jordin interjected. "Why don't you join me so we can talk?"

Lydia shook her head. "I didn't mean to interrupt your lunch…"

"You're not," she quickly assured her. "Please come with me. We have a lot of catching up to do."

"You are still that same little sweet girl, I remember."

Jordin unlocked the doors to her vehicle.

Once they were inside, she said, "Mrs. Holbrooke, I really think that you and Ethan should have a conversation, but he's not interested in doing this right now. Maybe he just needs more time."

"Jordin, I need you to understand that I never intended to just leave my son like that. I wouldn't have abandoned him. The only reason I went with Rob was because we were supposed to come back the next day. Things went terribly wrong."

"Ethan told me that you were in prison."

"I was," Lydia confirmed. "I honestly didn't know that Rob was trafficking drugs. I didn't even know he was a drug dealer."

Jordin met her gaze. "How could you not know? Even I had heard the rumors back then about Rob and so did Ethan."

"Because I believed in Rob," Lydia stated. "I was so in love with him at that time. He owned a couple of laundromats and I just figured they were very successful businesses. Back then any black man making good money was said to be selling drugs. It wasn't always true."

After parking the car, Jordin turned to Lydia and

asked, "So you really had no idea about the drugs in the car?"

"I didn't. Rob was even going to testify to this, but he died before he could. I was told that he had a heart attack while in jail, but through the grapevine I heard the cops beat him up pretty bad."

"I'm so sorry you had to go through this ordeal," Jordin stated.

"It was a hard lesson to learn but I survived. I just don't want to lose my son." A lone tear slid down her face.

"Ethan is under the impression that you knew about Rob and the drugs."

"This is why I need to talk to him."

Their conversation came to a pause until they were seated in a booth near a window.

"Mrs. Holbrooke, I need to tell you something," Jordin began. "Your son asked me to marry him and I said yes. Ethan and I are engaged."

Lydia broke into a smile. "I'm so happy for you both. I always knew that you would one day be my daughter-in-law."

"I'm relieved that you approve," Jordin said, picking up her menu.

"You're good for him."

"Order whatever you'd like. I'm buying."

"Jordin, you don—"

"This is my treat, Mrs. Holbrooke," she interjected. "My family's hosting an engagement party a week from Saturday. Why don't you come celebrate with us?"

"I don't know if I should come. I really don't want to upset Ethan."

"I'll get him to talk to you after the party," Jordin assured her. "He needs to know the truth of what happened. Once he knows the truth, then you two can get past this."

"When I heard he was back in Charleston, I was thrilled. I just want my son back in my life."

"I'll do what I can to help you."

Lydia embraced her. "Thank you so much, Jordin."

"You're welcome," she responded.

Jordin prayed she had done the right thing with inviting Lydia. Ethan really needed to sit down and hear his mother out. Maybe he would do so after the party.

The evening of the engagement party, Jordin and Ethan strolled hand in hand across the lawn of the Du-Grandpre estate, greeting guests as they made their way toward her parents. They both opted to celebrate their engagement at a casual yet elegant backyard cocktail party. Eleanor combined lush berry-hued florals and a black-and-white stripe motif for the decor.

"Mom outdid herself," Jordin said. "It looks beautiful."

When her grandfather's dogs strolled by wearing striped bow ties to match the theme, Ethan chuckled. "Yeah, she did. I think your parents invited the whole city to our engagement party."

Jordin gave a short laugh as his arms came around her. "It certainly looks that way. Are you sure you're ready for this, Ethan?"

He nodded. "We are going to be man and wife. I can't wait."

Jordin and Ethan both accepted a glass of champagne from a passing waiter.

"Here come the lovebirds," Jadin murmured with a smile. "I can't believe it. My sister's getting married."

Jordin embraced her sister. "I know... I can hardly believe it myself. I've never been as happy as I am now."

"I'm thrilled for you, sis. I really am."

Jadin turned to Ethan and said, "You take good care of my sister."

"I give you my word. I love Jordin more than my own life."

Ethan's expression suddenly turned to one of shock. "What is Lydia doing here?"

"She's here because I invited her," Jordin confessed.

"Why would you do this? You know how I feel about the woman."

"That woman is your mother, Ethan," Jordin said in a low voice. "Regardless of what has happened, she is and always will be your mother."

"It doesn't mean that I have to have a relationship with her."

"We are at a party to celebrate our engagement," Jordin stated. "We can discuss this later."

Chapter 21

"What could have possibly made you invite Lydia here?" Ethan demanded as soon as Jordin closed the front door of her home. "I thought I'd made it clear that I want nothing to do with her."

"She's your mother, for one thing," Jordin pointed out. "This is a very important moment for us and I thought it would be nice to have Lydia share it with us. The other reason I wanted her to come is because the two of you really need to talk."

"Lydia hasn't earned the right to share any part of my life, Jordin." A flash of disappointment streaked across his face. "I can't believe you would do something like this to me. You never once considered my feelings."

"Your feelings were the only ones I did consider, Ethan," she responded, folding her arms across her chest. "I invited her because I don't want you to look back one day with regret."

"I won't," he responded. "I feel nothing for that woman."

"I don't believe that," Jordin stated. "I know that you're angry and I'm not saying that you don't have a reason to be, but regardless of what you say, I know that your mother still matters to you."

"Hate is all I feel for her."

Jordin shook her head. "I don't believe that."

"It's true, I assure you."

"Well, I don't agree. I ran into your mother a week ago and we talked. There's a lot more to her story and it's something you really need to hear, sweetheart."

"I'm not interested," he uttered. "She can snow you with her excuses, but I'm not buying anything she has to sell."

"How can you be so coldhearted?" Jordin wanted to know. She studied him as if she had never seen Ethan before. "Are you still seeing Bree?"

"No, I didn't want to waste her time or mine. To answer your other question—I learned how to be cold from the best. *My parents.*"

"Ethan, your mother told me that she didn't know about the drugs."

"How convenient."

"I believe her."

"I don't," Ethan responded. "Jordin, as far as I'm concerned, I don't have parents. Please do not invite them to our wedding. Can you at least do that for me?"

"I don't know who you are," Jordin stated. "You are nothing like the boy I remembered."

"I'm a grown man," he responded. "I've changed over the years."

"I don't like what I'm seeing."

"I'm sorry to disappoint you."

"What happened to you, Ethan? Why are you so cold?"

He did not respond.

Jordin met his gaze. "Ethan…I don't think I can marry you." She removed the ring off her finger and handed it back to him. "I'm sorry."

"I can't believe this. You're choosing my mother over me?"

"That's not what I'm doing," she told him. "You are so angry and bitter."

"It has nothing to do with us."

"Yes, it does," Jordin countered. "I don't want this shadow hanging over our marriage."

"So what are you saying?"

"I don't think we should think about getting married right now."

"You're calling off the engagement?"

"Yes," she responded.

"I don't believe this," Ethan uttered. "Are you serious? You don't want to marry me because I have mommy issues?"

"What happens when we have a problem, Ethan?" Jordin inquired. "You don't forgive. There is no compromise with you. It's your way or none at all. This is not a quality I want in a husband."

"I appreciate your candor."

"I love you, Ethan. I have always loved y—"

"But you don't want to marry me," he quickly interjected.

Their gazes met and held.

"There is nothing else to discuss, then."

"Ethan…"

"Good night, Jordin."

She watched with tears in her eyes as Ethan stormed out of her house. This was not the way Jordin had imagined this night would end. They celebrated their engagement a few hours earlier and now they were no longer getting married.

With him gone, Jordin could not find peace in her own house because the memories of Ethan were too strong. She decided against sleeping in her bedroom because she could still smell him on her pillows.

Her guest room provided no comfort either. Throughout the night, Jordin dreamed of Ethan's arms around her, holding her tight, but she always awakened to the cold, empty spot next to her.

"Jordin called off our engagement," Ethan announced as he joined Chandler for lunch the next day.

"You two looked so happy at the party last night. What happened?"

"She took it upon herself to invite Lydia to the party. Jordin doesn't get that Lydia had a chance to be a mother, but she wasn't interested. Now I don't need or want that woman in my life."

"Jordin was coming from a good place, Ethan," Chandler stated. "The DuGrandpres are a close-knit family."

"I know, but that's not my story. Jordin works in family law, so it's not like she isn't familiar with dysfunctional families. She thinks that I should just forgive and move on."

"Sounds to me like you were pretty hard on Jordin."

Ethan did not respond.

"Are you sure you're ready to get married?" Chandler inquired.

Ethan eyed his friend straight on. "Jordin is the one who called off the engagement."

"Did you expect her to want to marry you after blowing up like that?"

"I wanted to make it clear that she was wrong to in-

vite Lydia to our celebration. I didn't want to share this
with that woman."

"I'm afraid that I agree with Jordin. You and your
mother will never work things out if you won't allow her
anywhere near you, Ethan."

Ethan sighed in frustration. "Why is this so hard for
you and Jordin to understand? I'm not trying to work
things out with her."

"Hey, I get it, but you can't hold on to this grudge
forever."

"I already went through this with Jordin. I mean it
when I say that I don't want Lydia in my life, Chandler.
Nothing is ever going to change that."

"I hope you don't come to regret this."

"I won't," Ethan uttered. "Now can we change the
subject?"

"Sure."

Although Chandler brought up another topic, Ethan's
mind was on Jordin. He could not help but wonder if he
had overreacted. He just wished she could understand
that it was not easy for him to forgive his mother. He
knew deep down that Jordin was right.

Ethan also could not escape the sadness reflected in
his mother's eyes each time he saw her. It haunted him
like a ghost that refused to leave. It bothered him, although he tried to reason that she had no right to feel
hurt by him—she was the one who tore his life apart.

"Why aren't you wearing your ring?" Jadin questioned. "I haven't seen you wearing it since the night of
the engagement party. That was a week ago."

"I gave it back to Ethan."

Jadin gasped in surprise. "When did this happen?"

"After the party."

"But why?"

Jordin met her sister's gaze. "Ethan and I decided that it was best to call off the engagement."

"I'm so sorry, Jordin."

She gave a slight shrug. "It's fine." The fact that she had not heard from Ethan bothered her. How could he claim to love her so much and not fight for their relationship? Her own heart and body were shouting at her to give him another chance—to give them a chance.

"Are you okay?" Jadin asked, propelling Jordin out of her reverie.

Jordin nodded. "I'm not happy about it, but I know that I made the right decision."

"You broke it off then."

She nodded a second time. "It's for the best, Jadin." Apparently, Ethan must feel the same way, Jordin thought. He wasn't making the situation any easier.

"You have been in love with Ethan for a long time. Are you sure about this?"

"Not really," Jordin confessed. "My heart feels as if it's been torn into a million pieces, but I have to believe I did the right thing."

"I never thought you were the type to just give up on someone," Jadin said. "Especially if it was someone you cared about."

Jordin eyed her sister. "I haven't given up on Ethan."

"He was abandoned by his parents. How do you think he feels about you right now?"

She considered her sister's words. "I suppose he may feel that I've abandoned him too." Jordin had made herself indispensable, fighting hard to become a part of Ethan's everyday life.

For the first time since that night, she questioned her decision to end the engagement.

Only for You

"I know that I was concerned that he would hurt you, sis, but now...I really think you and Ethan belong together."

"I know that we do," Jordin murmured. "But he's so angry with his mother. His heart is filled with unforgiveness. It made me wonder how he would treat me if we had problems come up in our marriage."

"I have to admit that I would have those same concerns," Jadin confessed, "but this is something you could address now."

"I only wanted him to sit down and talk to his mother so that it would be easier for him to move past the anger."

"He does have some valid concerns though, sis. None of which have anything to do with you."

"Not really, Jadin," she stated. "Mrs. Holbrooke told me that she had no idea that Rob was a drug dealer and she didn't know there were drugs in the car. Rob died before he could testify. He had some legitimate businesses and that's all she knew about."

"You believe her?"

"I do," Jordin responded. "Jadin, I could tell that she was telling the truth. If Ethan would just talk to her—he would see the same thing."

"Have you told him what she said?"

"Only that she didn't know there were drugs in the car. This is her story and I think she should be the one to tell him."

Jadin embraced her. "I need to get to the courthouse, but if you want to meet me for drinks afterward, give me a call."

"Okay," she responded.

Alone, Jordin took a deep breath, and pushed those thoughts out of her mind and tried to concentrate on her work, but Ethan insisted on sneaking into her head no matter how hard she tried to keep him out.

She lifted her coffee mug for a sip, then cradled the mug between her palms, letting the heat slide into her skin. *Maybe I should have just focused on the fact that I love Ethan and that he loves me.*

Now it was too late.

Chapter 22

Jordin needed to see Ethan. They needed to have one more conversation.

She left work and drove over to the house where he grew up. Jordin found him standing beside his car. She parked, got out and walked up to him, saying, "I had a feeling I'd find you here."

Ethan glanced over his shoulder. "Jordin, I didn't hear you walk up. How did you know I would be here?"

"I just figured you'd want to visit your childhood home at some point, so I just took a chance that it would be today."

"I don't know why I came here."

"It's a part of your past. I also heard that you purchased the house and have plans to renovate it."

"Chandler talks too much."

"I think it's really sweet that you want to do something like this. What are you planning to do with it?"

"Donate it to a family that needs a home."

"Really?" Jordin had assumed he would give it to his mother, but then again, considering his feelings toward Lydia...

Ethan nodded. "I hope that it will be filled with love and laughter."

"That's very sweet of you."

He turned and began walking toward his vehicle. "I thought you were still upset with me."

"I figured we needed to talk," Jordin responded.

He met her gaze. "You called off our marriage. What else is there left to say?"

"I'm trying to comprehend why you are being so stubborn about this. Lydia is your mother—the woman who labored to bring you into this world, Ethan. Don't you think she deserves a second chance to earn your trust back?"

"Jordin, I don't think you will ever understand what I went through," he responded. "I guess I don't understand why my relationship with Lydia is such a concern of yours."

"Because I love you. When you're in pain, I hurt also." She shook her head sadly. "Ethan, I can't believe you would say something like that to me. What happened to you?"

"There's something I haven't told you. Jordin, I hated being in military school. I ran away a couple of times. The last time, I begged my dad to let me come home. He did, but it didn't last long. I was out with my stepmother's nephew who was visiting at the time. We were at the mall and he tried to steal something. Anyway, we were stopped by security and they called my stepmother. When my dad got home, she and her nephew blamed everything on me. I was sent back to military school. My dad didn't even listen to me. I decided I was on my own from that point forward."

"I'm sorry you had to go through something like that." Jordin reached out, tracing the design of the iron fence. "It's clear to me that you would rather carry your anger as a badge of honor for the rest of your life. Well, I can't be a part of that."

"You've made that abundantly clear."

She sent a sharp glare in his direction. "I don't need your sarcasm, Ethan. This wasn't an easy decision for me. I came to see you because I wanted to see if there was still a chance for us."

"And so you've decided that what you don't need is a man like me."

"Don't put words in my mouth," she snapped.

"I don't want to argue with you, Jordin."

"Then don't," she responded. After a moment, Jordin added, "I love you, Ethan."

"I love you too."

"I'm not ready to give up on us."

Ethan met her gaze. "That's not what I want either, but…"

Jordin eyed the house. "I hope you didn't buy this house just to hurt your mother."

"Do you really think I'm that callous?" He paused a moment before continuing. "I guess you don't know me as well as you thought."

"Ethan, I talked to your mother and I still believe that you should have a conversation with her. It just may change the way you feel about her."

"Why don't you just tell me what Lydia told you? It must have been a good story for you to suddenly become her cheerleader."

"I wouldn't say I was her cheerleader," Jordin countered, "but I do believe her. Lydia is not without fault, but she is not what you think she is either."

"I have to go," Ethan uttered. "I don't have time for this."

Before walking away, he pulled her into his arms, kissing her. "I will always love you, Jordin."

The way Ethan said it almost sounded like a goodbye.

"What's wrong with you?" Ryker inquired. "You look like you've got something heavy on your mind."

Jordin shrugged. "I've been trying to reach Ethan since yesterday, but he's not responding to my calls or texts." She had not heard a word from him since their encounter at his childhood home.

"Did you two have a fight or something?"

"Things have been a little tense between us since I called off the engagement."

"Maybe's he just busy," Ryker offered.

"He could be really busy," she responded, "or he could just be ignoring me."

"It's obvious that you still love him, Jordin. Why did you break off the engagement?"

"At the time, I thought it was the right thing to do."

"And now?" Ryker inquired.

"I know it was the right thing to do. I love Ethan, but he is filled with so much bitterness… He is so angry, Ryker. I want so much to help him but he refuses to let me into that area of his life."

"This is something that he will have to work out, cousin. Ethan has to make the choice to live in the past or move forward."

"So what am I supposed to do?"

"Be with him," Ryker stated. "Be a part of his life. Show Ethan that you love him and want to be with him, flaws and all. Show him that you he can trust you. If you do all this—then you've done everything possible."

Ethan scanned his text messages from Jordin. She wanted to talk to him, but he was not ready to have another conversation with her about his mother. He read her last text and said, "I miss you, sweetheart."

Then call her, his heart whispered. Ethan had to find a way to prove to the only one who mattered to him that his love for her could withstand anything. He wanted to show her that he would never run from what they could have together.

After a moment, Ethan picked up the telephone and dialed Jordin's number.

"Hello..."

His heart skipped a beat at the sound of her voice.

"It's me," Ethan said. "I'm sorry for just getting back to you, but I've been busy."

"I'm sure you didn't relish talking to me either," she murmured.

"You're right," he admitted. "I didn't want to have another fight."

"Ethan, I don't want to fight with you. You should know that I'm not your enemy."

"It's important that you understand that Lydia is a subject we will never agree on, Jordin."

She released a soft sigh in resignation. "I suppose you're right, but I can't help but feel that you would feel differently if you just had one real conversation with your mom. I—"

He interrupted her by saying, "Jordin, I'm going to be out of town for a few days."

"Where are you going?" she inquired.

"Martinique."

"You do know that running away won't help the situation," Jordin uttered.

He did not respond.

"Ethan…" she prompted.

"I have someone waiting to see me, so I'll call you later."

He hung up before she could respond. Ethan was not going to allow her to try to convince him to talk to Lydia. He needed to get away and clear his mind. This trip to Martinique was so that he could do some soul-searching without any interruptions or distractions.

His future with Jordin depended on it.

Chapter 23

Ethan sat down on the beach and stared out at the ocean. He wished that Jordin was here with him, enjoying the island breeze. He had been there for two days already and missed her.

I can't believe we're fighting over Lydia. Why doesn't Jordin understand the pain Lydia caused me? Why it is so difficult to forgive her?

However, he had to forgive his mother because it was the right thing to do. Ethan hated seeing his mother living with her friend and nothing to her name. Although he felt that she deserved what she got—this was not the life he wanted for her.

Who was he to judge her?

Everyone made mistakes, including him. Ethan considered the mistakes he had made with Jordin, but she never once gave up on him. She loved him unconditionally.

Lydia was his mother—she gave him life and he owed it to her to hear what she had to say.

Ethan's eyes filled with tears.

Deep down, behind a wall of cement and hidden in the folds of anger was the love he had for his mother. With each tear, the wall came crumbling down. Years of pain ebbed and flowed as he sobbed. He took several cleansing breaths and wiped away his tears.

It was time to go home.

Jordin was surprised when she looked up to find Ethan standing in the doorway of her office. "Hey, when did you get back?"

"Last night." He entered, closing the door behind him. "I saw Ryker outside and came in with him. I hope you don't mind I just showed up here without calling first."

She gave him a tiny smile. "I'm happy to see you, Ethan."

"I had a lot of time to think when I was away. I came to apologize for the way I've been acting."

Jordin rose to her feet and strolled from around the desk. "Actually, I owe you an apology, Ethan. I shouldn't have pushed so hard to do something you weren't ready or willing to do."

"There's a lot I want to say to you, but I don't want to do it here. Can you come to my place tonight? We can have dinner and talk."

Jordin met his gaze. "Sure, I'd like that."

He smiled. "I'll see you later, then."

She watched him leave. There was something different about Ethan, but she could not put her finger on what it was—he was just different.

Jordin returned her attention back to her work. She planned to leave the office on time since she was going to have dinner with Ethan.

* * *

Ethan felt the nearly magnetic charge in the air when he opened the door to let Jordin enter. His gaze locked on her and when she smiled, everything inside him tightened. She had changed from the conservative black suit she had on earlier to a vivid orange dress with shoestring straps that snaked across her shoulders.

"As usual, you look amazing."

"Thank you," Jordin said.

He took her by the hand and led her from the foyer to the living room.

She sat down on the sofa.

"I'll pour you a glass of wine."

"Thanks."

He returned a few minutes later with two glasses of white wine and handed one to her before settling down beside her.

"I love you, Jordin. Sweetheart, I have loved you from the first day we met and I will never stop loving you. I just don't know if we can ever get past what happened... I honestly don't know, but there is only one way to find out for sure." Ethan set his drink on the marble coffee table without taking a sip.

"What's that?" she inquired.

"I need to speak with Lydia." He gave her a tight smile. "You were right all along."

"Are you sure about this, Ethan?"

He nodded. "I can't move forward if I don't settle this thing with my mother. I don't want to lose you, Jordin."

Jordin shook her head. "I don't want you to do this for me. Ethan, you have to do this for you."

"This *is* for me, sweetheart. I know from experience how life can change in a moment. I want to spend the rest of my days and nights with the woman I love—I don't want to waste any more time focused on the past. Jordin, you are my future."

She met his gaze. "Ethan, I can't see my life without you in it. These past two weeks have been so miserable. If you really want to meet with your mother, I want you to know that I support you fully. If you change your mind, I will still support you—we will get through whatever happens together."

He didn't want to waste another moment on being angry. Ethan was ready to grab hold of life with Jordin, and never let go.

Ethan kissed her hard, and then took a breath. "I almost messed this up completely. I just hope it's not too late."

Jordin responded by kissing him back passionately.

Desire ignited in the pit of his belly, the flames growing. Ethan struggled to fight the urge to take Jordin upstairs and make love to her. Pulling her closer to him, Ethan's lips covered hers once more, kissing her hungrily. "I'm so glad to have you back, sweetheart," he whispered.

"Being with you is all that matters. Wherever you are, as long as we're together—everything will be perfect."

"You're everything to me, Jordin."

"If you're still interested, I'd like to marry you."

He grinned. "We are definitely getting married, babe."

She held up her left hand and wiggled her fingers, prompting laughter from Ethan. He patted his pockets. "I think I left it at the office."

"The ring's not as important as you are to me," she responded as she wrapped her arms around him.

He embraced her, holding her tight. Ethan inhaled deeply, sucking in the light floral scent of her perfume. "I've missed you so much. To be honest, I've been miserable without you."

She kissed his cheek. "I missed you too. Ethan, I want to know that we can get through anything together. I need to know that you won't shut me out."

"I promise I will do better by you, Jordin. I give you my word that I won't shut you out anymore."

"Thank you," she responded. "We're good together, Ethan, but if you keep a wall between us, then our relationship or our marriage will suffer. I'm in this for better or worse. Before you put that ring back on my finger, I need to know that you feel the same way."

"I do," he told her, staring into her eyes.

He kissed her.

Jordin pulled away. "I don't want to eat blackened chicken, so I'd better get in the kitchen and check on dinner."

"I'm going to give Lydia a call."

She smiled. "I think that's a wonderful idea."

Chapter 24

"Thank you for seeing me, Ethan," Lydia said when they were all seated.

He glanced over at Jordin, then back at his mother. "I guess it's time we talked."

"Before you say anything, son, I want you to know that I had no idea about the drugs that were in the car. Rob told me that we were just going away for the weekend. I wanted you to come with us, but he said we needed some time alone. I found out about the drugs when the police in Maryland pulled us over."

"How could you be so blind?" Ethan wanted to know.

"I was in love and he had those laundromats, so I assumed that's how he made his money. He had them all over Charleston and Savannah."

Ethan shook his head in disbelief. "There were rumors about him."

"If I had known why he was really traveling to Maryland, I wouldn't have gone. I would've broken things off, Ethan. I need you to believe me."

He did not respond.

"After I was arrested, Rob was going to testify that I had no knowledge of the drugs in the car, but he had a heart attack before he could do it."

"How do you know this?" Ethan inquired.

"My attorney told me, but without his actual testimony... I had nothing to help my case."

"You were innocent."

Lydia nodded. "I was naive, Ethan. I was in love, and I believed him. It was a foolish thing, I know..."

"You paid a heavy price for love," he muttered.

"Losing you was the worst of all," Lydia said tearfully. "I love you so much. Being away from you all this time was the hardest to bear."

Ethan could see the sincerity in her eyes and his heart felt her pain. "I'm sorry you had to go through all this."

"Your forgiveness is all that matters to me. I hope that you will be able to give me that one day."

"I forgive you," he responded. "I didn't know what you were up against. I need you to forgive me for the way that I've treated you. I was wrong."

Lydia began to cry. "I've waited so long."

Ethan wrapped his arms around her. "Mom, I've missed you so much," he whispered. "Even while I was so angry, I missed you. I just couldn't admit it."

Lydia touched his cheek lovingly. "Son, I understand."

Jordin wiped away a lone tear that slipped down her face. She was thrilled beyond words to witness Ethan's reunion with his mother.

"Despite everything, you turned out a great man and I'm so proud of you."

"Are you still staying with your friend?"

Lydia nodded. "I have a little job now, but it doesn't pay enough for me to have my own place."

"Mom, I want you to move into the guesthouse out back. It has two bedrooms, one and a half baths…it's perfect for you."

Lydia glanced at Jordin. "You two are getting married. How do you feel about this?"

"It's a great idea," she responded.

"I'll let you and Jordin decorate the place," Ethan said with a smile.

"I am grateful to have a place of my own. I'm sure it's fine the way it is." Lydia wiped away more tears. "I can't believe this is really happening."

"It can use some fresh paint and you're going to need furniture, Mom. Until your place is ready, I'd like for you to stay with me," Ethan told her. "We have a lot of catching up to do."

"I'm good with administrative work. Is there anything I can do to help you out with your business?" she asked. "I'd like to earn my own keep."

He broke into a smile. "Mom, you don't ever have to worry about working again. We'll go to the bank to-morrow to set up an account for you. We will also get you a car."

"This isn't why I wanted back in your life, Ethan," Lydia stated firmly. "Your love is all I really need."

"You're my mother. I realize now that you didn't abandon me—it was the other way around and I want to make it up to you. I told you when I was twelve that one day I would take care of you. I mean to do just that. You were an innocent woman sent to prison. It's time for you to enjoy your life."

"I agree with Ethan," Jordin interjected. "I am on the board of a couple of charities and we could use some additional help. We have a huge event coming up, so we really need you."

"I would love to do whatever I can," Lydia responded. "As for a car, I don't need anything fancy—just something to get around town."

He hugged her. "That's why I want you to choose your own vehicle. We could never agree on cars, remember?"

Lydia laughed. "I like Honda and he liked Toyota."

Jordin smiled as she listened to the light bantering between Ethan and his mother. He was happy. She could see it in his eyes as well as the affection he felt for Lydia. Gone was the mist of anger that once resided in his gaze. The walls that were once erected around Ethan's heart had collapsed, weakened by love.

"You were right all along," Ethan told Jordin when he returned after dropping off his mother. "I should have listened to you."

"You needed to come to this conclusion on your own," she responded. "Ethan, I'm so proud of you."

"So you really don't mind having my mother live here on the property with us?"

Jordin shook her head no. "She needs a home of her own. I think it's perfect because you two need to make up for all the time you missed."

"That's why I love you."

She broke into a sexy grin. "Is that the only reason you love me?"

He leaned forward and whispered in her ear, prompting Jordin to laugh. She picked up a pillow and hit him with it.

"Hey, that's one of the reasons you love me," he said.

"I don't know...it's been a while," she responded.

Ethan picked her up and carried her to the bedroom. "Let me remind you."

Eight months later

Her wedding day was finally here!

Jordin stood outside surrounded by fourteen acres of live oak groves and peaceful views of the Ashley River, on Lowndes Grove Plantation. She and Ethan had chosen this beautifully restored setting for their wedding because of its scenic sunset views of the waterfront. The Main House boasted a 1786 construction, period furnishings, a stunning expansive piazza and sun-kissed terraces made of bluestone, brick and oyster tabby. It was the perfect backdrop for Ethan and Jordin's June wedding.

She smiled and carried her travel tote into the Main House.

"Here you are…" her mother said. "I was worried that you were running late."

"No, I was outside just admiring the view."

"Everything is ready," Eleanor announced. "Your dress is upstairs."

"Before I get ready, I want to peek into the room where the ceremony will be held."

She followed her mother into one of the banquet rooms.

The rows of seating were garnished with lavish displays of purple-and-ivory flowers arranged with peacock-green-colored ribbons and baby's breath.

Smiling, she said, "It's perfect."

Eleanor embraced her. "It's time for you to start getting ready, my darling."

Jordin checked her watch. "I'll see you in a few."

She walked briskly up to the second level.

"I was just about to drive over to your house," Aubrie announced when she entered the dressing room.

"I'm here."

Her bridesmaids were all dressed in platinum-colored designer gowns. On a nearby sofa lay a row of beautiful hand-tied blooms in colors of purple, ivory and green.

"Kiera is ready for you," Jadin announced, referring to the hairstylist.

Jordin hummed softly as she sat down in the empty chair in front of Kiera. She could hardly believe it was her wedding day. She and Ethan were getting married— it was a dream come true.

An hour later, Jordin stood in front of a huge full-length mirror eyeing her reflection.

"You look so beautiful," Jadin said as she approached her sister. "I can't wait to see Ethan's face when you walk down that aisle."

"I can't believe that this day is finally here," Jordin gushed.

"I'm so happy for you, sis."

Jordin smiled. "Thank you."

Eleanor entered the room wearing a flowing gown in a deep purple color. "Oh, my…" she murmured. "There are no words to describe how beautiful you look…" She dabbed at the corners of her eyes.

"Please don't cry, Mom," Jordin pleaded. "I don't want to ruin my makeup."

"I love you."

She smiled. "I know and I love you too."

Eleanor hugged her once more. "I'll see you soon."

"Can you all give me a moment?" Jordin asked her bridesmaids. "I just need a few minutes alone."

Jadin embraced her. "You look so pretty, sis. Mostly, you look very happy."

"I am," Jordin confirmed. "I can't put into words just how happy I am right now."

"We'll be outside when you're ready."

When she was alone in the room, Jordin walked back over to the full-length mirror. She smiled at her reflection. In a few minutes she would be walking down the aisle toward her future. Jordin closed her eyes and sent up a silent prayer of thanksgiving. God had truly blessed her and she would be forever grateful.

Her father opened the door and peeked inside. "It's time," he said with a smile.

"I'm ready," she responded as she retrieved her bouquet.

"I love you and I'm so very proud of you." He gestured toward the door. "Now let's not keep your husband-to-be waiting."

She grinned. "That has such a nice ring to it."

Moments later, Jordin floated down the aisle on her father's arm toward the man she would love forever.

They stood facing each other as they said their vows.

Jordin could hardly contain her excitement as she waited to hear the words that would make their union real to her.

"I now pronounce you man and wife…"

Ethan exhaled a long sigh of pleasure. He pulled Jordin into his arms, drawing her close. He pressed his lips to hers for a chaste, yet meaningful kiss.

The room exploded into applause.

They walked down the aisle and through the double doors to the hallway.

Ethan's eyes traveled down the length of her, nodding in obvious approval. She was an ethereal vision in an elegant, backless dress with lace sleeves. Soft curly tendrils framed her face while the rest of her hair was pulled into an upswept style. "You look so beautiful, sweetheart."

Jordin broke into a big smile. "Can you believe it?

We're married." She held up her left hand as if to show off her wedding rings. "This is the happiest day of my life."

After the photographs, the bridal party made their way to the room where the reception was being held.

The talented event planners hired by her mother had put their magical touch on the space and filled it with more beautiful flowers, tables draped in plum-colored linens and elegant chandeliers hanging from above. Jordin noted how artichokes were tucked into the arrangements, the grayish-green color of the vegetable picking up the color scheme exquisitely.

"Everything is perfect," she told Ethan in a low voice. "My family…your mother is here. Your father and your siblings—this was absolutely the best day ever."

He agreed. "I wasn't sure my dad would come, but I'm glad he did. You know, the planner your mother hired really did a wonderful job." Ethan glanced over his shoulder. "Whose idea was it to have our guests write notes on fabric swatches?"

"It was actually mine," Jordin responded. "I love quilts and so I thought it would be unique to have the messages from everyone made into a quilt for us."

"It's a great idea."

Guests had a choice of four entrees, two vegetables, rice pilaf and an assortment of dinner rolls. After Jordin and Ethan finished eating, they navigated around the room, personally thanking everyone for attending the celebration.

It was soon time for the bride and groom to have their first dance.

Ethan only had eyes for Jordin. "I love you, sweetheart. With every fiber of my being, I love you."

"I love you back," she told him.

Next, Jordin danced with her father while Ethan led

his mother to the dance floor. Seeing them together like this pleased her to no end.

The night wore on. When the clock struck ten, Ethan asked, "Are you ready to leave?"

Her lips turned upward, thinking of what was to come. "Yeah. Let's get out of here. You go say goodbye to your mother and I'll say goodbye to mine."

Ethan shook his head. "You're my wife now, sweetheart. We'll take time to say goodbye to our combined family together. We are all family now."

"You're right."

"Jordin, are you leaving now?" Amya wanted to know. "Me and Kai want to dance with Ethan."

"I wouldn't miss out on dancing with you two beauties," Ethan responded.

Jordin sat down at their table smiling as she watched her husband with the girls. Kai and Amya were having a ball.

"He is going to be a great father," Jadin commented.

Jordin nodded in agreement. "I think so too. He is so good with the girls."

She glanced over and saw her mother talking and laughing with Lydia as if they were old friends.

Ethan returned to the table with Amya and Kai in tow.

"Did you see us dancing?" Amya asked.

"I sure did," Jordin responded. "I even had the photographer take some photos for our wedding album."

"I don't want you and Ethan to leave," Kai stated.

"We have to leave because we are flying out early tomorrow morning for our honeymoon."

"We can't go on the honeymoon with you?" Amya wanted to know.

"If you go with us, who is going to be here to play with your little brother?"

"Mommy and Daddy can play with him," Kai replied.

"Yeah," Amya contributed.

"Honeymoons are for the bride and groom," Ryker said when he joined them. "It's long past time for little girls to go to bed, so we're leaving now."

"I'm not sleepy," Kai complained before stifling a yawn.

Jordin pulled the little girl into her arms. "I'll be back next Saturday, okay?"

"Kay…"

"Are you gonna bring us a present from the honeymoon?" Amya asked.

"Of course we are," Jordin responded.

She reached over and gave Amya a hug as well. "Little girls need their beauty sleep, so I'll see you later."

"They are so lovable," Ethan said when the girls left with their father. "I think they already have me wrapped around their little fingers."

Jordin agreed. "They're my babies."

"You know…I think we should consider starting a family sometime next year."

Surprised, Jordin glanced up at Ethan. "Are you serious?"

He nodded. "I am. I want to have some children of my own, especially a little girl."

"You don't want a son?"

"I'd like one of each actually," Ethan stated.

Jordin couldn't stop grinning. She could not believe how much he had changed since reconnecting with his parents. Ethan and his father were building a relationship and were planning their first father-son trip together in the fall. She was thrilled for him.

"What?"

"Ethan, I love seeing you like this. I feel like we're whole now."

"That's because you complete me, Jordin."

Austin walked up to the table. "Do you mind if I borrow my sister for a moment? I need to talk to her."

Jordin could tell by his facial expression that something was wrong. "I'll be right back, honey."

"Austin, what's wrong?" Jordin asked when they walked over to the bar.

He responded with a question of his own. "Are you and Bree Collins close?"

"She and I have been friends since our freshman year in college. Why?" She could not imagine why Austin would have a problem with Bree. "How do you know Bree?"

"She has a son, right?"

"Yes…" Jordin glanced over her shoulder to where Bree was sitting, then back at him. "She adopted him last year." Comprehension dawned. "Are you saying… No…"

"She has my son."

"Austin, I'm so sorry."

He met his sister's gaze. "I know that she's your friend, but Jordin, I'm not going to let her keep my son. I never would've agreed to an adoption if I'd known about him."

"Please don't confront her here."

"I'm not going to do anything to ruin your wedding day."

"She adores little Emery." She paused a moment before continuing. "Austin, she's a good mother. Can you just get to know her before you say anything?"

He shook his head. "Too much time has passed already."

"Please…just get to know her. I think it would be best

for your son. You can't just walk in and take him from the only mother he's ever known."

"I suppose you're right, Jordin." After a brief pause, he said, "Okay, I'll do this your way. I only ask that you keep this between you and me for now."

"You have my word."

"This means you will have to keep a secret from your husband."

"I believe he will understand," Jordin responded. "I'm sure of it."

"You and Austin were deep in conversation," Ethan stated upon her return to their table.

"We were discussing Bree."

He broke into a smile. "Really? Is he interested in her?"

"Yes," Jordin responded. "He wants to get to know her better."

"I'm not a matchmaker, but I think they would make a great couple."

She glanced over at her husband. "I was just thinking the same thing, but I suppose only time will tell."

"Enough about them. I want to focus all of my attention on you. I am a lucky man, Jordin."

She broke into a smile. "I know… I'm just glad you recognize it."

"My heart has always belonged to you, sweetheart."

"Same here," Jordin responded. "My heart has always been reserved only for you."

* * * * *

REQUEST YOUR FREE BOOKS!

2 FREE NOVELS
PLUS 2 FREE GIFTS!

KIMANI™
ROMANCE

Love's ultimate destination!

The porch light flickered, casting the area in shadows. She'd been meaning to change that bulb.

"Thanks again," she said, getting her keys out of her purse.

Jacobe took her elbow in his hand and turned her to face him. He stood so close that she had to tilt her head even farther back to meet his gaze. In the flickering light of the porch, she couldn't make out the expression in his eyes.

"I respect your honesty, Danielle." His other hand came up to brush across her chin. "Don't think this kiss means otherwise."

KPEXP0117

Her heart fluttered and anticipation tingled every inch of skin on her body. "Who said you could kiss me?"

His dark eyes met hers and the corners of his mouth tilted up in a sexy smile. "Tell me I can't and I won't."

The air crackled around them. Sparks of heat filled her chest. Her eyes lowered to his lips. Full and soft. Based on the smoldering heat in his eyes, his lips desperately wanted to touch hers.

"One kiss," she whispered.

Don't miss FULL COURT SEDUCTION
by Synithia Williams, available February 2017
wherever Harlequin® Kimani Romance™
books and ebooks are sold.